DANNY ORLIS
AND THE
OLD MINE MYSTERY

DANNY ORLIS

AND THE

OLD MINE MYSTERY

BERNARD PALMER

Please note that several books in the Danny Orlis series are published by Sword of the Lord Publications and are available for purchase on their website, www.swordbooks.com.

Aneko Press Youth

www.anekopress.com

Aneko Press, Life Sentence Publishing, and our logos are trademarks of Life Sentence Publishing, Inc.
203 E. Birch Street
P.O. Box 652
Abbotsford, WI 54405

JUVENILE FICTION / Religious / Christian / Action & Adventure

Paperback ISBN: 979-8-88936-028-5

eBook ISBN: 979-8-88936-029-2

10 9 8 7 6 5 4 3 2 1

Available where books are sold

CONTENTS

CHAPTER 1

DARLENE'S PLAN

Kay Orlis looked up with concern.

"Are they going to send you down south for the summer, Danny?" she asked.

He nodded. "I've got to go down to Central America to help overhaul three or four aircraft. I'll probably be gone until the first of September." He read the fear in her eyes. "It's just routine, Kay," he assured her. "I won't even be doing any flying to speak of while I'm gone."

"I wasn't thinking about that. It's Kent that I've been concerned about. How will I manage him without you?"

"That's what I've been thinking about. He's paroled to me. I'm responsible for his conduct."

"And I don't think I can handle him alone," she replied. "I couldn't do anything with him before he got arrested with Jack Ross and that Riley guy for attempting to rob the warehouse. I don't know whether I'd be able to do anything with him now or not."

Danny's forehead crinkled.

"I thought perhaps my parents might keep him up at the Angle for the summer, Kay."

"Oh, I'd hate to see you send him up there. I know they'd take him and do their best with him, but neither your dad nor mother has been feeling so well lately. I'm afraid the responsibility for a boy as wayward and defiant as Kent would be too much for them."

"I've been thinking about that, too." He shook his head doubtfully. "I just don't know what to do with him, Kay. It's a real problem."

"We'll have to make it a matter of prayer, Danny," she replied.

* * *

That afternoon Kay and Danny were surprised by Ron and Darlene who drove over from Cedarton for the weekend.

"It's really good to see you both," Danny said, pumping his younger brother's arm vigorously. "Kay and I were talking about you last night. We were wondering if we were going to see you before I head South for the summer."

"Where are you going, Danny?" Darlene could not hide her disappointment.

"I'm flying down to Central America for a few

weeks." He eyed her curiously. "But I'll be home before you and Ron are to be married the last of August."

"The last of August?" She turned to Ron. "Didn't you write to Danny and Kay about our change in plans?"

His lean face colored.

"I was going to, but you know how it is. I kept putting it off and–."

"Maybe you'd better tell us all about this," Danny said, picking up one of the suitcases.

At that moment Jim Morgan came running up.

"Hi, Ron. How're you doing?"

Ron grinned and rumpled Jim's hair affectionately.

"Ron! Am I glad to see you! I've been planning to write to you to see if you could come over and visit us. The fishing's been great around here ever since the season opened. We've got some brand-new spots that're just waiting for a couple of good fishermen to try out. How about going over there with me the first thing in the morning–." His voice broke off as he saw Darlene. "Oh." The light faded from his eyes. "I see you brought *her* along."

"Sure thing."

Jim scowled. "I was hoping that you and I could get in some good fishing on this trip, but I guess we'll have to give it up."

Darlene spoke up quickly. "I don't know why we can't. I like to fish too."

"You?" Jim's lips curled in disgust. "Who ever heard of taking a *girl* fishing?"

They went into the house and Darlene sat down across from Jim.

"Now," she said, eyes dancing, "I want to talk to you, Jim. Just what've you got against taking me along?"

"We'd probably have to bait your hook for you and everything."

"Darlene isn't like just any girl," Ron said. "I've taken her fishing lots of times. She'll hold her own against most of the guys I've fished with."

Jim turned to him. "Tell me something. Did you put the minnows on the hook for her?"

"Well, yes."

"But not because he had to," Darlene broke in.

Pointedly Jim ignored her.

"And did you have to land her fish for her?"

"I don't know that I had to, but I did."

"Did you take her fish off for her and put them on the stringer?"

1 guess so.

"And when you got back, did you clean them for her?"

"Sure, but–."

"Boy, if you say that's like fishing with another guy, all I can say is that you've got it a lot worse than I ever thought you did."

Danny entered the conversation abruptly.

"I think you may as well give up, Jim," he said. "I think Ron has got it 'pretty bad' as you say – bad enough, in fact, to be here to make wedding plans."

Jim stared at Ron incredulously.

"You don't mean it. You've got to be kidding."

Darlene laughed. "Am I as bad as all that?"

"Oh no." He answered quickly. "You're OK, Darlene – for a girl. But getting married–." He wrinkled his nose.

"You'll still be here the first of the month, won't you, Danny?" Ron asked.

"I'm supposed to leave about that time. As I recall, I'm due in Central America July 1."

"You could delay your trip until after the second, couldn't you?" Darlene asked.

"I'll sure check on it."

While the Orlis brothers and Jim were talking a few minutes later, Kay and Darlene scooted their chairs together and began to go over the plans for the wedding.

"Just listen to them," Danny said, jerking his head in their direction. "I think the three of us might just as well go fishing tomorrow morning. I don't think they'll even miss us."

Jim brightened.

"Now you're talking."

* * *

That evening after Jim, Kent, and Jill were in bed, Danny told Ron and Darlene about Kent and the problem they faced with him.

"If I were going to be home this summer, we wouldn't be concerned at all. He'll mind me after a fashion. But he's more than Kay can manage."

Ron thought for a moment. "I don't suppose it would work out to send him up to the Angle and have them take care of him."

Danny shook his head. "We talked about that, but I'm afraid it would be too much for them. Kent's harder to handle than even Jim was when he first came to live with them."

Darlene spoke up.

"I don't actually know Kent very well," she said, "but it would seem to me that a good Christian boys' camp might be something to consider. A place where they would have good supervision coupled with Christian training."

Danny and Kay looked at one another.

"That sounds like our answer, Danny."

"The problem would be to find a camp that would take him. Not many of them would want to have the responsibility for a boy who's been in as much trouble as Kent has."

"I don't think that's too much of a problem," Ron offered. "There's the camp our cousins, Bob Anders and his wife, are directing this summer. The way I get it they take quite a few problem guys."

"Is Bob going to be at a boys' camp this summer?" Danny asked. "I thought he was working with the Indians in Ontario."

"He stopped at Cedarton about six weeks ago on his way back to Colorado," Ron replied. "His health hasn't been too good, and the doctors thought a year or so in a milder climate would help him. So, he's moved his family back to Colorado and has taken over the directorship of Wild River Canyon Boys' Camp."

"It sounds good."

Ron told Danny and Kay something of the history of the camp, how it had been organized, and the way the director and counselors worked with the boys. When he finished, Danny's gaze met Kay's.

"That sounds wonderful, doesn't it, Kay?"

"It's an answer to prayer!"

CHAPTER 2

KENT'S REACTION

Jim got up early Saturday morning hoping he could coax Danny and Ron to go fishing with him. Ron was game, but Danny had other plans.

Jim's lower jaw sagged. "You mean we can't go fishing after all?"

"You and Ron can go, but something's come up that I've *got* to do. Sorry."

"But Danny!" The boy's voice rose. "This is practically the last time Ron'll have to go fishing with us – as a free man."

"Well, maybe I can go this afternoon," Danny conceded, "if I get through with what I've got to do this morning."

He telephoned Judge Lee who had heard the case against Kent and asked for an appointment. Ron went with him to the judge's house about 9:30, and Danny told Judge Lee the situation with Kent.

"I quite agree with you," he said when he had heard Danny out, "Kent is no lad for a woman to try to handle alone."

"That's why we thought about this camp in Colorado."

Judge Lee took a pencil from his pocket and toyed with it momentarily.

"It sounds like a good solution to a difficult problem," he said at last, "and I have no objection to your placing him there for the summer. But do you think they would take Kent?"

Danny turned to his younger brother. "You were the one who talked with Bob about their camping program, Ron. What do you think?"

"I couldn't speak for them, of course," Ron replied, "but I do know they take a certain number of problem boys. Bob told me that several judges in Denver regularly refer boys to them for the summer."

Judge Lee smiled.

"Ever since you've been talking, I've been thinking about the other boys who were involved in this incident with Kent. They need something like this too. I'd like to send all three of them."

Danny called his cousin in Colorado and got permission to send all three boys there for the summer.

"Of course," Danny said, repeating what Bob had said to him, "they can't make any definite promise that they can help the boys. All they can do is present the claims of Christ to them and show them that He loves them. Whether or not they accept Him is up to them.

And if they don't, there's very little they can do for them."

Judge Lee nodded. "But at least they won't be on the streets of Fairview for the summer. It will be that much to the good."

When Danny and Ron returned home, Danny talked with Kent about camp. Suspicion lit the boy's eyes.

"What's the trouble?" he demanded. "Are you getting tired of having me around? Or didn't you mean it when you told the judge you wanted me to stay with you?"

"Of course we meant it," Danny said. "But I'm not going to be here this summer, and Kay and I thought you'd enjoy going out to Colorado to camp while I'm gone."

"Enjoy it?" Derision curled his lips. "I ain't lost nothin' out there."

Ron spoke up.

"I've heard all about this camp, Kent, and it's great. You'll love it."

Kent's eyes blazed defiantly. "Let me clue you in on somethin', buster! I ain't goin'!"

Danny ignored his use of poor English. "I want to make something clear to you, Kent. It doesn't really matter what you think about going to camp. You're going anyway."

"We'll see about that!"

"The judge has already approved it," Danny said evenly. "All three of you boys are going."

"All three of us?"

"Lee Nelson, Walt Thatcher, and you."

Kent flushed. "Now, whose big idea was that, havin' those characters go along?"

"The judge thought of it."

"It would be bad enough goin' there alone," Kent continued. "It'd be terrible goin' with those guys."

* * *

That evening Bob Anders called Danny and asked if he could furnish a counselor for the summer. Danny called Boyd Patterson first, but he already had a summer job lined up. Tom Channing, however, was excited about going.

"You know, Danny," he said, "since I yielded my life completely to God and decided to go into full-time Christian service, I've been concerned about what I was going to do this summer. I–I'll pray about it and–and talk to Dad, but I think you can count on me."

"Good. Get in touch with me as soon as you can, will you?"

"The first thing in the morning."

Jim came into the living room as Danny put his phone in his pocket.

"Danny," he said, "how about letting me go *to* that camp with those guys as a counselor."

"I'm afraid it wouldn't work, Jim."

"Why not?" He sat down and leaned forward intently. "I've been to camp lots of times."

"You're a couple of years too young for one thing," Danny told him. "But in this case, there's something else that's hindering you. Something even more important than your age."

Jim frowned his disappointment.

"Frankly, Jim, you don't have the heart for it."

"What do you mean by that?"

"You don't have real compassion for the lost."

"There's where you're wrong, Danny," Jim retorted. "I've done more witnessing at school than just about anyone I know. All the kids know where I stand."

"That's fine, Jim, but it's not exactly what I'm talking about." He paused momentarily. "Tell me, have you been praying for Kent? Have you been asking God to touch his heart so he can be won for Christ?"

"Well–" Jim swallowed hard, and crimson crept up into his cheeks. "I–I–."

Kent came swaggering in just then. Belligerence was flaming in his eyes.

"I don't need nobody to pray for me," he blurted. "I'll get along all right. And I ain't goin' to no stupid old camp, so you can just start thinkin' of somethin' else to do with me."

"The matter is settled, Kent," Danny said quietly.

"I ain't goin'! Now, what d'you think of that?"

Danny got to his feet.

"Kent," he said quietly, "go to your room."

The boy's chin sagged. "For cryin' out loud!" he exploded. "Can't a guy even talk around here?"

"Not like that. Go to your room and stay there until you think you can speak respectfully to me."

There was a short, tense silence while their eyes met and fought savagely. Kent turned at last and went into the bedroom, closing the door behind him.

Jim spoke quickly.

"What good does it do to pray for a guy like that?" he demanded. "That's what I'd like to know."

"He's lost, Jim." There was real compassion in Danny's voice. "Just the way you and I were before we confessed our sin and accepted the Lord Jesus Christ as our Savior."

Jim was still sitting there staring into space when Kay and Darlene came into the room twenty or thirty minutes later.

The next morning shortly after Danny and the others got up to get ready for Sunday school, Danny's phone rang and he answered it.

"This is Tom Channing. I just talked to Dad. He thinks going to camp as a counselor is a great idea!"

* * *

On his way back from one of the Canadian mission stations a short time later, Danny stopped at Angle Inlet and picked up his parents. They planned to spend a few days visiting in Fairview before the wedding.

"I wish we could be in Minneapolis for all the showers and parties they're having for Darlene, don't you, Mother?" Kay asked.

The older woman smiled. "That would be nice, but I'm just happy that we're able to be at the wedding and that Ron is marrying such a lovely Christian girl." She paused. "You know, Kay, Dad and I thank God every night for both you and Darlene. You'll never know how we've rejoiced that both of our sons have chosen such lovely, considerate Christian girls."

They were still talking when Danny and his dad came in. Carl was smiling broadly.

"Don't tell me what you two were talking about," he teased. "Let me guess."

Mary Orlis wrinkled her nose at him.

"I suppose you think we were talking about the wedding."

"Well, weren't you?"

She hesitated.

"In a way."

"That's just what I figured."

He and Danny crossed the room and sat down.

"I wish I were certain that I could be at the wedding," Danny said.

Both his mother and Kay straightened suddenly.

"Not be there?" Mary echoed. "Danny, you just can't miss Ron's wedding. It will ruin everything if you're not there."

"I don't want to miss it, believe me," he replied.

"I was talking with the people at the mission about it today and asked if I could delay my trip for a few days, but I haven't had final word on it yet."

"But they're getting married next week, Danny," Kay said, indignation rising in her voice. "Surely they understand that you don't want to miss the wedding."

Danny sighed.

"They understand, all right. It's just that a couple of the planes that are badly needed are out of service. I feel an obligation to the missionaries down there. If a short delay won't cause an emergency, I'm sure they'll give me permission to wait."

CHAPTER 3

KENT'S NEW FRIEND

Danny got permission from the board to wait to go to Central America until after the wedding. The day before Ron and Darlene were to be married, he was up at dawn and out at the airport long before anyone else was around. He was busy checking out the mission's Cessna 180 when his dad drove up.

"I'm glad you're able to stay until Ron and Darlene are married," Carl said, standing nearby while his son worked. "We'd all have been disappointed if you'd had to miss it."

"I talked with Dr. Gordon about it. He didn't think the delay would hurt anything. And besides, I've still got a little time off coming from last year's vacation."

Carl went over to the toolbox, selected the wrench Danny needed, and handed it to him.

"I wish I could stick around until you and Mother have to go back to the Angle," Danny told him.

"Now don't give a thought to that. It's much more important that you get that aircraft in good operating condition than it is that you hang around here visiting with us."

"I guess you're right, Dad."

There was a short silence.

"Danny," his dad said, "I thought I'd come out and see if you'd like to have Mother and me drive your car to Minneapolis today, so we'd be able to bring Kay and Jim back here after the wedding."

"Sounds like a good idea."

Danny continually kept the aircraft in good shape, so it was a comparatively simple job to check it out. By nine o'clock he was certain everything was in order and ready to go.

When he and his dad got back to the house, the rest of the family was gathered in the kitchen. Mary, Jill, and Kay were sitting at the table.

Kay got to her feet as the door opened. "I didn't think you'd be back so soon, Danny."

He sat down at the table across from his mother.

"It didn't take too long this morning."

They ate lunch at 11:30 and shortly after noon they were ready to start for the Twin Cities. Jim went with Danny to the plane.

"At least there's one good thing about Ron getting hitched," he said. "I'm getting another plane ride."

* * *

The following evening Ron and Darlene were married in a small suburban church near the Snyder home. Danny was the best man and Kay was the matron of honor.

Kay was with the bride in a small room off the main sanctuary helping her with her gown. Darlene laid a restraining hand on Kay's fingers momentarily, and her face grew pensive.

"There's only one thing that could make today more perfect than it is," she said softly, "that is if Roxie were here."

Kay nodded in understanding.

"You know, Kay," she went on, "Roxie and I always said that we were going to be the maid of honor at each other's wedding."

A smile lit Kay's face.

"I know how you feel, Darlene," Kay said. "And I'm sure that nothing would have made Roxie happier than to have had you marry Ron. You were her best friend, and he was her twin brother."

There was a brief silence and for an instant a tear trembled on the young bride's eyelashes.

"I wonder why the Lord had to take Roxie home, Kay?" she asked. "I just can't understand it."

"I'm sure we'll not know the full answer to that question until we get to heaven, Darlene," Kay told her, "but we can be sure of this. There was a purpose. A very real purpose. The Bible says, 'And we know that God causes all things to work together for good to those who love God, to those who are called according to His purpose.' "

Darlene's lips quivered.

"I know two things that happened because of it," she said. "Ron got back into the center of God's will, and I got my life straightened out for the first time as far as consecration is concerned."

"I'm sure that's not all that happened. I'm sure that it had a big effect on many, many people, including Danny and me."

At that moment Mrs. Snyder opened the door.

"Darlene, are you ready?"

"I think so."

"I do declare, I believe I'm a lot more excited and nervous about this than you are."

Darlene laughed happily.

"It just shows a little more with you, Mother."

Kay glanced at her watch.

"Perhaps you'd better go out into the foyer so you can be ushered in, Mrs. Snyder. The music should be starting in a few minutes."

Darlene smiled radiantly at her mother.

* * *

At dawn the next morning Danny Orlis kissed his mother and Kay goodbye and took off for Guatemala. For a moment or two Kay stood there watching the plane with tears in her eyes.

"I should be used to having Danny go away and leave me alone," she said to no one in particular. "It happens often enough since he's been flying for the mission. But I don't think it's any easier now than it was the first time it happened."

Mary put her arm about her young daughter-in-law's shoulders.

"I know just how you feel. But just knowing that Danny is serving the Lord makes it so much easier."

Kay nodded, smiling brightly through the tears.

* * *

Tom Channing sat back in the bus seat and closed his eyes. Kent, who was in the seat next to him, stirred restlessly.

"How much longer is it goin' to take to get there?" he asked.

Tom opened one eye and glanced at his watch. "We should be there in four or five hours."

Kent sighed deeply. "I don't know why I'm in such a hurry to get to that stupid camp. We're goin' to be stuck there for the whole summer."

Tom did not reply. Kent's voice raised.

"Of all the dumb ideas, this one tops 'em all! Imagine, gettin' stuck at a *Bible* camp all summer!"

Tom sat up and half turned to face him. "It's not going to be so bad."

"That's what you think!" His face reddened angrily.

"I'd just about as soon have gone back to that orphanage, and I ain't kiddin'!"

Tom and his young charges had to change to a southbound bus in Denver to go down to Colorado Springs. It was only an hour's ride to the thriving little city in the shadow of Pike's Peak. When they got out at the bus depot, the sun was still high overhead.

Kent walked to the corner and looked about, a sneer marring his young features.

"How far did you say it is up to that camp?"

Tom shrugged.

"Twelve or fifteen miles, I suppose."

"And just how're we supposed to get there?" Disgust was heavy in every word.

Tom started to answer but checked himself as a young man about Danny's age came striding up to them.

"Are you Tom Channing?"

"That's right."

"My name's Bob Anders." He shook hands with Walt, Lee, and Kent. The first two greeted him warmly, but Kent only scowled in return.

Bob led them across the street to a station wagon. When they got there, Walt and Lee were piled into the back seat with their luggage. Kent had no choice but to get in front between the camp director and Tom.

"I'm sure you guys are going to be glad you came here," Bob said.

"Don't go to bettin' on that!" Kent sneered. "I've got to stay at your goof-ball camp, but I don't have to like it."

Walt spoke up. "Maybe Kent won't like it, Mr. Anders. He doesn't like a lot of things. But Lee and I think it's great to be comin' out here."

"That's for sure," Lee added.

Bob drove out of Colorado Springs and, heading almost directly west, passed Pike's Peak and drove off the highway to the left. Lee, who had been staring in silence at everything around them, leaned forward and tapped Bob on the shoulder.

"Do you ever see any deer up here, Mr. Anders?"

"We often have them right in camp."

Lee's eyes widened.

"And that's not the only kind of wild game we have here in Wild Horse Canyon. We've got bear, elk, a few wolves, and mountain lions, to say nothing of the porcupines, beaver, and small game."

Walt expelled his breath slowly.

"I'd like to come up here hunting. That's what I'd like to do."

"Maybe you can someday."

Bob drove slowly past two cabins and crossed the Wild River to stop in front of the administration building. "Well," he said, "here we are."

The grounds were cleared only enough for the cabins and facilities it took to operate the camp. Winding paths led from the administration building to the sleeping cabins, the dining hall, and the chapel. Beyond the big log chapel was a swimming pool and to the other side a large clearing that served as a baseball diamond.

Walt whistled his amazement.

"I've never seen anything like this before."

Lee was staring in the direction of the big barn.

"What's that big barn for, Mr. Anders?"

"That's where we keep our saddle horses."

"Do you mean you've actually got horses for us guys to ride?"

Bob laughed. A moment later he turned to Tom. "Maybe you'd better have the boys get their gear, Tom. And I'll show you your cabin."

The three boys looked at Tom with new respect. Bob didn't spell it out to them, but they knew what he was telling them. He was reminding them that Tom was in charge. Tom was getting the message, too. Bob expected him to handle the boys in his care, to see that they kept the rules and did not get hurt.

Tom turned to Kent and his companions.

"All right, guys. We'd better go up to the cabin and get our stuff put away. It won't be long until dinnertime."

At the cabin they were introduced to the other two boys who were to be with them. Kent sized them up carefully. Dick Shafer was quite a bit older and bigger than he was. However, Bruce Mackay was smaller and younger. He was more the sort of guy Kent would be able to make friends with. While the others were unpacking their suitcases and getting their clothes put away, Kent sidled up to Bruce.

"Hi."

The smaller boy eyed him. "Hi yourself."

"Where you from?" Kent asked.

"Denver. How about you?"

Their eyes met.

"A lot farther than that. I live in Minnesota."

Bruce's eyes widened in surprise. "What're you doing at camp way out here?"

Kent grimaced. "It ain't my idea. I can tell you that much."

"You won't find it so bad," Bruce replied, "after you get used to it."

Kent motioned with his head for Bruce to follow him and started slowly for the door. Bruce fell into step beside him. When they were outside a dozen yards or so from the cabin, he turned to Kent curiously.

"What's the big idea getting me out here?"

"Think they can hear us?"

Bruce shook his head.

"I haven't been here an hour yet, and I'm fed up with this dump already. Don't think they're doin' all this for us because they like us. They can't kid me. They've got an angle."

"What do you mean?"

"You just watch. They've got their reasons." Kent lowered his voice. "This is just to hook us so they can shove their religion down our throats."

Bruce turned that over in his mind.

"But you 'n' me are goin' to have some fun, Bruce. We ain't goin' to let 'em get their hooks into us."

Bruce eyed him once more.

"I–I don't know whether I want to go along with you or not, Kent," he said hesitantly.

"What's the trouble?" Kent demanded. "Are you scared?"

"I've been in enough trouble already. I–I just don't want to get anybody else on my neck."

Kent laughed. "We ain't goin' to get into trouble. We're just goin' to have some fun. We'll show 'em a thing or two!"

CHAPTER 4

DOC'S LOST GOLD MINE

During the next several days the boys were kept so busy at camp they scarcely had time to think about anything else. They swam, hiked, and fished for trout in the stream that skirted the campgrounds. They had lessons in first aid, handcraft, and lifesaving. And, of course, they attended Bible lessons, messages, and testimony times. To Kent's surprise, he found that he was enjoying himself a great deal although he would have fought with anyone who dared to say so. He expressed himself loudly at every opportunity. It bothered him particularly that Walt and Lee seemed to like camp so well.

"You mean to tell me that you *like* this dump?" he asked them, lips curling.

Walt swung his feet over the side of the bed and sat up. "You can say all you want to against the camp, Kent," he retorted. "But you're not going to change my mind. This place is the greatest."

"Hmph. Just wait 'til they start pourin' the heat on you about religion. You won't think it's so great then."

Lee crossed the room and sat down near the window. "I don't know," he said. "I even like the Bible lessons."

Derision tinged Kent's youthful face.

"They've already got you hooked, and you don't even know it."

He would have said more, but Tom came in just then and called them together for their evening devotions.

When they had finished reading the Bible and Tom had led in prayer, the boys lingered for a few minutes around the table. Tom looked from one to the other.

"Well," he began, "you haven't been here at camp very long, but I can't help wondering how you stand with God." He paused significantly. "Have you confessed your sin and put your whole trust in Christ to save you?"

There was a long silence. Walt took a deep breath and cleared his throat.

"Did you have something you wanted to say, Walt?" Tom asked.

The boy's cheeks darkened slightly, and an embarrassed little laugh escaped his lips. "I was just going to say that I don't know whether I've put my whole trust in Christ to save me or not."

Tom did not register surprise.

"If you don't know for sure, there's a very good chance you aren't right with God," he said, "that you've never confessed your sin and put your whole trust in Him for salvation." Tom spoke softly, but with a confidence that seemed to radiate from him.

Kent caught Walt's eye and smirked knowingly. Walt flushed.

"I–I–."

"Have you been giving thought to the claims Christ has on your life?" Tom continued.

Walt started to answer but glanced in Kent's direction and checked himself. When he spoke, he was strangely evasive.

"I don't think I care to go into it any more tonight," he said, changing the subject abruptly.

As the guys went over to their bunks, Kent jabbed Walt knowingly in the ribs and spoke to him in a whisper.

"It's a good thing for you I was here! That's all I can say."

The color rushed to Walt's cheeks.

Tom prayed for Walt for a long while that night before going to sleep. The boy had seemed so close, so very close, to making a decision for Christ. If only he had been able to talk with him alone!

The following day Tom tried to maneuver Walt into a conversation once more, but the boy evaded it warily.

* * *

That night the boys were helping to build the fire for the evening service when they had a visitor. A grizzled old mountaineer came up on horseback. His horse was a gaunt, spavined old bay, as crippled with rheumatism as he was. He rode up to Bob and reined his mount.

"Howdy, Bob," he said.

"Doc Staughton!" Bob exclaimed. "What are you doing over here?"

"Nothin'." He dismounted and dropped his horse's reins to the ground. "Ain't no law again' that, is there? I just got lonesome, so I figgered I'd ride over and sit for a spell."

"Fine. You're just in time for our campfire service."

Kent, who had been listening intently ever since the mountaineer rode up, approached him quickly.

"Want me to tie up your horse for you?"

That seemed to influence Doc. A crooked grin twisted his face. "Nope. Ain't no use to tie up Maggie. She ain't goin' nowheres." He sat down on one end of a big pine log. "When my grandpappy first came out to these here hills, you wouldn't have started no fire like that." His voice cracked. "Not and keep your scalp on your head, you wouldn't. The Injuns woulda seen it twenty miles away."

Lee moved closer. "Do you remember when the Indians used to be out here?"

Doc wiped at his watery eyes with the back of a gnarled fist.

"I seen my share o' Injuns, and that's fer sure. But I can't recollect havin' seen any on the warpath."

Disappointment dulled the lights in the boys' eyes.

"Nope," he continued, "but my old grandpappy, he seen plenty. The fact is, it was the Sioux what kilt him! Right in these here mountains! An' they skinned the hair offen his head the same as you'd peel an orange."

By this time the old mountaineer had the attention of everyone. The boys crowded close about him in a silent semicircle, listening intently. He leaned forward on the log and lowered his voice.

"My grandpappy didn't know much about the mountains when he first come West and settled out here, but it wasn't long 'til he could find his way 'round like an Injun. He was a regular mountain man."

Walt broke in. "Why'd he come out here?"

Doc shrugged his shoulders. "T' find gold, just like everybody else. And find it he did. Leastwise, my pa said he come home one night with a sack of nuggets that'd choke a bullfrog and a story of a vein of gold so pure the assayer wouldn't b'lieve his test."

The boys' eyes widened, and their lithe young bodies grew tense with excitement. Lee asked the question that was foremost in every mind.

"Did your grandpa get to work his claim?"

"Yep," Doc said. "He worked it for a couple of years an' woulda made a fortune for all of us if it hadn't been for the Sioux. They went on the warpath and kilt my grandpappy. I wouldn't be surprised none if his scalp didn't end up on old Crazy Horse's shirt."

"What did you do then?" Lee asked.

"Me?" Doc echoed. "I didn't do nothin'. I wasn't even borned yet."

Laughter tittered across the tense crowd of listeners.

"What did your father do then?"

"He didn't do nothin' either. He was just a little shaver." He measured a short distance from the ground with his hand. "My grandmammy was so skeered she wouldn't go traipsin' out to no mine alone, so 'bout fifteen years or so went by b'fore airy a Staughton went to look for it."

"Did they find it?" Walt asked.

The old prospector shook his head.

"Nope. My pa spent the best years of his life a-lookin' for that mine, an' I've been a-roamin' over these here hills myself since I was knee high to a short-legged jackrabbit, and neither one of us ever seen nairy hide nor hair of it."

Kent had been listening in silence, but now he spoke up, awe tinging his voice.

"You–you mean it's still lost out there?"

"It sure is. Leastwise, nobody's found it since I been nosin' around these here hills."

"Wouldn't it be somethin' to find a gold mine?" Kent exclaimed.

Bob, who had been listening to the conversation, chose that moment to step forward.

"I know you guys have all been interested in what Doc Staughton has to say. I've been interested myself. But it's time for our campfire service to begin."

Kent groaned audibly.

After the campfire service that evening the guys walked back to their cabin together. Kent called Bruce to one side.

"What did you think of that old buzzard who came over to visit camp tonight?"

"That was really something!"

"Wouldn't it be great to find a gold mine?"

"You can say that again." The corners of Bruce's mouth tightened. "Only how could we find it? He's been looking for it for years."

"We just might be the lucky ones," Kent said. "If we could sneak over to his cabin and get him to talkin', we might get some leads on where to start lookin' and things like that."

"We couldn't do that," Bruce countered. "We're not supposed to leave camp!"

"Just let me take care of that! I'll think of somethin'!"

Kent and Bruce laid out their plans for looking for the old mine very carefully. They got together to talk about it every chance they had. And with each passing day their excitement grew.

"We've got to find out where the mine is supposed to be," Kent said guardedly. "We can't go to roamin' all over the mountains lookin' for it."

"How're we going to find out anything about where it is?" the other boy wanted to know.

"I've just got a hunch old Doc Staughton might give us some clues," Kent continued, "if we go over and get to talkin' to him."

That very afternoon during free time Kent sought out Bob Anders and engaged him in a discussion about the old mountaineer.

"I sure did like him," Kent said.

Bob chuckled. "Yes, most everyone finds him interesting."

Kent hesitated. "Does–does he live around here?"

"Just up the mountain half a mile or so." Bob went on, "He has an old shack where he's been living for the past thirty years while he roams the hills hunting for his grandfather's lost gold mine."

Kent wanted to locate Bruce right away and get over to the old-timer's shack, but by the time he found his new friend, it was time for the afternoon meeting to begin.

"You aren't planning on sneaking away now, are you?" Bruce asked, looking anxiously toward the chapel.

"There isn't time."

Kent was glad they had gone to the meeting that afternoon although at the time he'd been disgusted with Bruce for not being around in time for them to sneak from the camp. As it turned out Bob Anders himself was at the meeting, and he was one of those guys who didn't miss a thing. If they'd sneaked out on the meeting, Bob would've certainly known it.

Walt, who was sitting near them in the chapel, fidgeted uneasily. Kent saw that the laughter had gone out of his eyes and his usually carefree face was somber.

At the dinner table that evening Walt didn't say

much. When the meal was over, he went off by him-self. Kent saw him leave and followed him.

"What's the matter?" he taunted. "Is the preachin' gettin' under your hide?"

Walt whirled to face him. His eyes were blazing. "You shut your big mouth!"

Involuntarily Kent took half a step backward.

"I–I didn't mean nothin'."

Walt's voice raised belligerently. "You'd better not, that's all I can say! If I catch you lippin' off to anybody, I'll tear your head off your shoulders!"

Kent would have continued to tease him, but Walt stood half a head taller and was thirty pounds heavier than he was. He turned and went in search of Bruce.

When time came for the evening campfire service, Walt didn't want to go. He went over to his counselor.

"I don't feel so good, Tom."

"Maybe you'd better go over to the infirmary and let the nurse look at you."

"Oh, I'll be all right," he replied quickly. "I just want to lie down for a while, that's all."

"I can tell you what's eatin' him," Kent smirked, "if you really want to know."

Walt glared at him.

When the guys came back from the campfire service that evening, he was sitting on his bunk, his chin cradled in his hands.

"Hi, Walt," Tom said. "How're you feeling?"

"All right, I guess." His voice was heavy.

Tom got his Bible and started to lead them in their devotions. Walt came over to the table hesitantly and stood for a moment looking down at Tom.

"I can't take part in devotions tonight!" he blurted, fear and desperation edging his youthful voice.

"Why not?"

"I–I'm not a Christian."

Tom's gaze met his. "That's a serious matter, Walt, but it's something that can be remedied. In fact, you can take care of it right now."

Walt nodded miserably.

"I can't go on the way I have been. I've sure made a mess out of my life."

Tom got to his feet quickly.

"Let's go down to the chapel where we can be alone."

The other boys stared after them somberly. It was a long while before anyone spoke. Kent was the first.

"They finally got to him!" he snorted in derision. "I told him it'd happen, but he wouldn't listen to me! An' now they got him!"

Lee's lower lip quivered.

"I don't think he'll ever be sorry."

A few minutes later Bob came into their cabin and conducted the devotions in Tom's place. Tom and Walt still weren't back by the time the boys were to be in bed.

Kent crawled into his bunk. He was lying awake when Walt and Tom reentered the cabin. He lay there, silently staring up into the darkness and listening as they talked in low tones while preparing for bed.

"You know, Tom," Walt was saying, "this is something I've been wanting to do ever since I first got here and saw how different the guys who're Christians really are."

Kent rolled over on his side and closed his eyes. He knew exactly what Walt meant. He had been feeling the same thing. He felt it even now. He had gotten into all kinds of trouble back in Fairview, and he had determined he was never going to let anything like that happen again. But he knew, even as he made himself such promises, that it wasn't going to work out. Not unless he had what Walt and Tom had.

He rolled over and sat up in bed.

"Tom!" He spoke softly. "Tom!"

CHAPTER 5

ESCAPE!

There was a long, breathless silence. Kent lifted himself on one elbow and spoke urgently once more. "Tom!"

But there was no answer.

"Tom!"

For half a minute he waited tensely. If only Tom would wake up!

He sat up straight and swung his feet over the side of the bunk. In an instant he could have Tom awake and get the matter settled. He hesitated. If he did wake Tom up, the chances were that everyone else in the cabin would wake up too. And if that happened, he'd be the laughingstock of the camp, especially after the way he had ridiculed Walt. Every guy he knew would be on him. And he couldn't have that.

Reluctantly Kent got back into bed and closed his eyes. He'd talk with Tom first thing in the morning. He'd get him off alone somewhere and ask him for help.

Kent tried to sleep, but every time he closed his eyes, he could hear Walt's earnest voice. He should have wakened Tom. He realized that. But it wouldn't be long until morning now. That wouldn't be too long to wait.

Although Kent lay awake most of the night, he finally drifted off to sleep near morning. He was sleeping soundly when the bugle called the camp to life.

"Hey, Kent," Bruce called. "Wake up. You're going to be late for breakfast."

Slowly Kent got out of bed and began to dress. Tom had already gone outside and was sitting on the front steps with the rest of the guys from the cabin nearby. Kent frowned. Now he'd have to wait until after breakfast to talk to Tom.

When the breakfast bell began to toll, the guys rushed up the path. Kent jerked his shirt off the nail where he had hung it and hurriedly pulled it on.

"Bruce," he called, "wait for me!"

But his new friend hurried out the door. Kent followed, still buttoning his shirt. Tom had started with the others but looked back and saw Kent. For some reason he stopped and waited.

"Hurry up."

Kent felt the color sneak into his cheeks. It had all seemed so easy the night before to think about talking with Tom about the Lord Jesus. He had even planned exactly what he was going to say. But now that he was with Tom, he was uncertain about what to do. Things seemed so different in the daylight. For some reason salvation didn't seem to be so important at the moment.

Tom talked with him about Walt on the way to the dining room.

Kent's mouth firmed. "Maybe that's best – for him!" His voice rose angrily. "But I don't need that stuff. I can get my life straightened out on my own!"

They reached the dining hall and Kent scooted inside away from the counselor.

When they had finished breakfast, Bob had devotions for the entire camp.

"Before we have our Bible reading this morning," he began, "I wonder if there is anyone here who would like to give a word of testimony."

He didn't look in Walt's direction, but the instant he stopped speaking Walt got to his feet.

"When I came here, I decided I was going to have fun, but I wasn't going to get mixed up in this religion business," he said. "So, the first week I kept my ears closed to the messages, the lessons, and that sort of thing."

He took a long breath and glanced seriously about the dining room once more.

"But I couldn't keep my eyes closed to the way some of you guys lived. I saw that you were different than I was. You looked as though you were having a lot of fun, but you didn't break the rules. You had an attitude I didn't have."

His smile widened, and joy leaped high in his eyes.

"So, last night I confessed my sin and gave my heart to Christ. And I can tell you guys who haven't done the same thing that you don't know what you're missing."

A breathless hush settled over the big dining hall.

Kent's face whitened, and for an instant his lips quivered. Bruce was breathing heavily.

"I never heard anything like that before," he whispered.

"Just wait awhile," Kent said derisively. "He's talkin' big, but you ain't seen him livin' it yet."

Bruce swallowed hard. "He sure sounds like he means it."

"It won't last. I guarantee it!" But even as Kent spoke, doubt crept into his voice. Like Bruce said, Walt sure sounded as though he meant it. But it wouldn't last. It couldn't!

As soon as devotions were over Kent pushed back from the table and got to his feet.

"Come on, Bruce."

"Where you going?" Bruce asked hesitantly. "I–I think maybe I'll stay in here for a while."

Kent faced him belligerently. "Who do you want to talk to? Tom or Bob Anders?"

The boy's face flushed, but he stared defiantly at Kent. "What's it to you?"

Kent took him by the arm and started toward the door.

"Come on! Don't fall for that stuff. If you do, we won't get to go see Doc Staughton or anything."

Still Bruce hung back. "I–I want to get my life straightened out the way Walt did."

Kent stared at him, eyes blazing.

"All right! But if you do, just remember you and I are through!"

Bruce acted as though he was about to leave, but he checked himself. Kent threw back his shoulders.

"You can go and talk to one of those guys this afternoon or tomorrow. Right now, I've got something planned."

"About?"

"Come on!"

Reluctantly Bruce left the dining hall and walked rapidly away from everyone else.

"I've just been thinking," Kent said in a taut whisper, "this is the day we should go see Doc Staughton."

Excitement gripped Bruce. "Do you think we can do it without getting caught?"

"The way I've got it planned it'll be a cinch." Kent glanced over his shoulder and back again. "Meet me by our cabin in twenty minutes."

"But that's the time our Bible lesson starts."

Kent laughed.

"Where'd you rather go? To listen to a dumb old Bible lesson or over to see Doc Staughton and find out something about that gold mine?"

Bruce's body tensed.

"Do you think he'll tell us anything that might give us a lead on the mine?"

"If I didn't, we wouldn't be wastin' our time goin' over there."

Twenty minutes later the boys disappeared around the corner of the cabin and into the brush. They crept quietly up the steep slope and across to the stream that bisected the camp property. Every half minute Bruce glanced over his shoulder.

"Think they heard us?" he asked uneasily.

"Not a chance. If they had, we'd have been grabbed a long time ago."

"But what're we going to do about sneaking back into camp?" Bruce wanted to know. "How're we going to keep away from Bob and the counselors then?"

"We'll worry about that later."

They crossed the stream and the main camp road and dipped into a narrow ravine. Kent led Bruce up the other side, heading almost due south until they came to a narrow, winding trail that led up the mountain.

"Here we go, Bruce," he said. "Now there wasn't much to that, was there?"

"We're not back yet."

They continued up the mountain toward the little log cabin where old Doc Staughton lived alone. It was a long, difficult climb that seemed much longer than the half mile Bob said it was. Once or twice, they stopped to rest.

"We shouldn't have left camp the way we did, Kent," Bruce said. "We broke about every rule they've got. We're probably in real trouble."

"We can't be in trouble," Kent countered. "They don't even know we're gone."

There was a brief, taut silence. Bruce laid a hand on his pal's arm.

"Come on, Kent," he said. "Let's go back."

Kent straightened indignantly.

"Go back?" His voice raised. "After we're this close? Don't be stupid!"

"But–."

"Listen, I've about had it!" Kent leaned forward and lowered his voice. "I wasn't going to tell you this, Bruce. Tom asked me not to. But I'm goin' to let you in on it so that you'll know what the score is." Kent spoke evenly as though he was telling the truth. "Tom said that Bob didn't really mean anything by that little speech about rules. Sure, they don't want all the guys running every which way all over the mountains, but they don't care if a couple of guys go off by themselves for a couple of hours or so."

Bruce turned the matter over in his mind.

"If that's the way it is, why didn't we go and get permission from him?"

Derision gleamed in Kent's eyes.

"Don't you see? If we'd gone to him for permission, he'd have to turn us down. But this way he'll just pretend that he doesn't know about it and everything'll be all right."

That seemed to stop Bruce's objections. They went on to the tiny cabin where the old, gray-haired prospector lived alone. When they reached the clearing on the banks of the mountain stream, Doc was sitting on a stool just outside his cabin door mending a well-worn bridle.

"Howdy!" A smile brightened his lined face. "Come on over and sit awhile."

For a minute or two he eyed them critically.

"You guys are from the camp, ain't you?"

The color crept up into their cheeks.

"Yep," Kent lied easily, "we talked to Bob Anders, and he said we could come up and see you if we wanted to."

A smile lifted one corner of Doc's mouth. "Now that was right neighborly. I never knowed him to do that before."

"We did some special work for him," Kent replied lamely, "and when he found out we wanted to see you, he said we could come."

Doc stood painfully.

"Come on in the cabin." He led them into his little log building and had them sit down in the rough, handmade chairs. "If I'd knowed you was comin' I'd have tidied up the place a mite."

"We were sure excited about that gold mine you were tellin' us about the other night, Mr. Staughton," Kent said.

"Most boys is interested in knowin' about that mine." He chuckled to himself. "What're you aimin' to do, slip out an' find it for yourselves?"

Bruce started to reply, but Kent cut in quickly with still another lie.

"We wouldn't try anything like that. It belongs to you."

Staughton shook his head. "No, it don't," he said. "It b'longs to whoever finds it. That's why I've got to be sorta careful 'bout what I tell to people. Someone might find out what I know and locate that mine, just like that." He snapped his fingers. "But I don't know why I'm worried 'bout anyone else findin' it. I been a-lookin' fer it all my life, an' I ain't found it yet. Course, some greenhorn just might come along an' find it first crack out of the box."

As they talked, he began to tell them things that had happened to him as he searched for the mine. He mentioned places where he had looked and the places he felt were still worth exploring.

"I don't know why," he said at last, "but I've got a sneakin' hunch the mine's somewhere on this very mountain. That's why I moved over here thirty years ago." The light in his eyes all but died. "But I've walked every inch of this here mountain a dozen times, an' I ain't never come across nothin' yet that looked like no gold mine."

The boys were so interested in what Doc Staughton was telling them that they forgot what time it was until suddenly Bruce jumped to his feet and ran to the window.

"Kent," he exclaimed, "do you see where the sun is? It's going to be dark in an hour!"

"Maybe we'd better be goin'," Kent said, getting to his feet.

"You c'n ride my horse if you want to," Doc said. "She'll go good double. That way you'll get home in just a little while. I c'n come by and pick her up in the mornin',"

Kent was almost to the door. "No, we can't do that. I mean, we don't want to put you to all that trouble."

And before Doc could say any more, they were out in the yard. They hurried across the clearing to the little path that led down the mountain. Bruce looked at his watch.

"We're really in for it, Kent," he said. "They've missed us by this time for sure."

Kent quickened his pace. "I still think we can sneak back into camp without being seen."

They had walked and run most of the way back to camp when Bob and Tom came into view.

"There they are!" Bob exclaimed.

"And just who gave you permission to leave camp?" His voice was like ice.

Kent Gilbert looked at Tom and then back to Bob helplessly. It was no use to lie now. He knew that much.

"I–I–"

"You're both apt to be on your way home in the morning."

CHAPTER 6

BOB'S DECISION

Lips trembling, Bruce clutched at Bob's sleeve. "You–you wouldn't really send us home, would you?"

"Can you think of any good reason why I shouldn't?"

Kent broke in quickly, fear tinging his voice. "We didn't mean to be gone very long," he said. "To tell you the truth, we didn't plan on being gone more than a few minutes, but we–we–" He thought fast. "We got lost."

Bob's eyes narrowed.

"I'm not sure that I buy that, Kent," he said. "But if you were lost, that's all the more reason why we have to punish you." His voice raised. "Just why do you suppose we have rules against leaving camp?"

"My dad'll skin me alive if you send me home from camp for breaking the rules," Bruce choked miserably. "He'll skin me alive!"

Bob's expression did not change.

"That's something you should've thought of before you sneaked away." He turned on his heel. "Come on. We've got to get back to camp before they send everyone out to look for you."

Bruce started to speak again, but Bob strode with quick, sure steps down the mountain toward camp. The boys followed along behind.

Bruce glanced at Kent.

"I told you we shouldn't have sneaked away from camp the way we did, Kent." He spoke softly and with a quavering voice. "I told you we'd get caught and be in bad trouble if we skipped out on the Bible lesson."

Hostile eyes fastened on him.

"Pipe down, will you?" Kent demanded.

"You don't have to be as scared of getting sent home as I do," Bruce continued. "If they don't let me stay at camp, I'm going to be in an awful jam."

Kent's anger flared. "It ain't goin' to be no worse for you than it is for me. Now, lay off! I've about had it!"

They walked on in silence. Every once in a while, a dry sob escaped Bruce's throat.

It was dinnertime when they finally got back to camp. Bob sent Bruce and Kent directly to their cabin, however.

"Ain't we goin' to get nothin' to eat tonight?" Kent asked, self-pity curling his lips.

"I'll have something sent over for you. I don't want you to be with the rest of the guys until we decide what we're going to do with you."

The muscles in Bruce's face twisted nervously.

"You don't have to have anything sent over for me," he stammered. "I–I don't think I'm hungry."

Bob turned to Tom.

I'd like to have a talk with you, Tom."

Tom nodded. Before they left, Bob turned once more to Bruce and Kent.

"And you guys had better be here when we get back. Is that clear?"

The boys were left alone.

Bruce stared after Bob and Tom until they disappeared from view. Then he went into the cabin and stood uneasily by his bunk.

"What do you suppose is going to happen to us, Kent?" he asked.

Kent threw himself face down on a bunk across the room.

"How should I know?"

Bruce picked up his Bible and thoughtfully fingered it. "If we'd done like Walt did, we wouldn't be in a mess like this." He was speaking more to himself than to Kent.

Kent rolled over on his back and sat up. "You aren't goin' to fall for that stuff, are you?" Contempt was written bitterly on his face.

"Walt sure seems to be a lot happier than he ever was before."

"That's what he says."

Doubt gleamed momentarily in his eyes. "Isn't it the truth?"

Kent swung his feet over the side of the bunk. "It's just a front he's puttin' on. He got himself into a peck of trouble back home, and he figures that somethin' like this will help him to take the heat off a little bit."

"He told about the trouble he's been in when he gave his testimony," Bruce countered. "The way I got it, that was all settled. He'd been put on probation or something."

"That's what *he* says. I know different."

"But Tom lives in the same town you guys do," Bruce continued. "He'd know if Walt wasn't telling the truth."

Kent came over to him.

"That's part of Walt's scheme," he said. "Tom's one of the guys he's tryin' to fool."

But Bruce stood his ground. "He didn't act as though he was tryin' to put anything over on anybody."

"All right!" Kent's temper flared. "If you want to get taken in by that religious bit, go ahead. Go to Bob and make a fool of yourself if that's what you want to do. But, if you do, don't plan on bein' in with me on our gold mine deal. You and me are through."

Bruce swallowed hard.

"If they send me home, I'll be through anyway."

There were heavy footsteps on the cabin porch, and Tom came in with something for them to eat. Kent took his sandwich and began to wolf it hungrily, but Bruce pushed his aside.

"What're you guys going to do to us, Tom?" he asked fearfully.

"Mr. Anders will decide that in the morning."

"Is–is he going to send us home?"

"You'll have to ask him, Bruce. All I can tell you is that he's very angry with you guys." Tom sat down on a bunk. "You know, running away the way you guys did was sure a stupid thing to do."

A sneer marred Kent's young face. "We can get along without any sermons from you."

"Before I became a Christian," Tom said quietly, "I used to feel the same way when I thought someone was going to talk to me about the Lord."

Kent came back and sat down on the bunk across from him.

"All right," he blurted at last. "Get it over with."

"What do you mean?"

"You're not goin' to be satisfied until you've given me a Bible verse and a little message about how bad I am."

Tom shook his head. "No, I don't think it would do any good to talk with you about Christ tonight," he said.

His answer surprised Kent, but the boy did not let on that he was surprised. "Now you're gettin' smart."

"You're belligerent and arrogant tonight," Tom told him. "And you've steeled your heart against anything that might be said to you."

For an instant the words drove to the very depths of Kent's being.

"It ain't goin' to do you no good to preach to me tonight or any other night. You ain't got nothin' I want!"

In spite of Kent's open belligerence, he tossed

restlessly on his bunk that night. The following morning, he got up half an hour before the rest of the guys, dressed quietly, and slipped out behind the cabin until they had all gone to breakfast. Bruce was sitting at the table reading his Bible when Kent returned. As the screen door opened, he slammed the Book shut and scooted it off the table to his lap.

"Think readin' that is goin' to do you any good?"

The other boy said nothing, but his face turned bright red.

"You should wait 'til Bob comes up to talk about sendin' us home. If he sees you readin' your Bible, he just might change his mind about you."

Bruce's eyes flashed. "That's not why I was reading."

Kent laughed. "Ease off, guy. You don't have to play games with me. I ain't goin' to squeal on you. Go right ahead. Make 'em think you've changed and're goin' to be a good boy now. I'm for you if you can get away with it."

Bruce went outdoors and stood until Bob came to talk to them. The camp director came brusquely into the cabin and had the boys sit down.

"You both know you broke the rules, don't you?" he began sternly. "You know I can send you home, don't you?"

"Yes, sir." Fear and respect mingled in Bruce's young face.

"Is that what you want?"

Both boys shook their heads. For the moment, at least, Kent's arrogance was gone.

"I don't want to send you home, either, because we want to try to help you. But these regulations are for your own protection and for the protection and welfare of the others. Anyone who stays here must obey them."

Bruce broke in quickly.

"I'll never do it again, Mr. Anders. If you'll just let me stay, I'll never leave again without permission."

Bob's manner did not change.

"You've broken our rules," he said, "so there must be some punishment. But if you will give me your word that you'll never leave camp again without permission, we'll give you both another chance."

Relief flooded Bruce's face.

"Oh boy!" he exclaimed. "That's great."

"You might not be so happy when you hear what your punishment is to be."

"Oh, that won't make any difference. All that counts is that we get to stay here."

Bob turned to Kent. "And what about you? How do you feel about it?"

Kent's eyes lit up. "I feel the same as Bruce does. I sure don't want to have to go home."

"That's good." There was a brief hesitation. "Of course, it all depends on you. If you want to stay here badly enough to obey regulations and live up to our restrictions to the very letter, everything will be all right. But–." His face grew stern. "If you break the rules just once more, you'll have to go home. Is that clear?"

"You won't have to worry about us anymore," Kent assured him. "We won't give you any more trouble."

"You can say that again," Bruce put in. "We've learned our lesson."

"For your sakes, I hope that's true."

He outlined the restrictions that were placed upon them. They were placed on work detail for two hours each day. They were not to go swimming or horseback riding or to take part in any of the extra activities.

"We're not going to set any definite time limit on the restrictions," Bob said. "It will all depend on how well you live up to them and what your attitude is."

When he was gone Kent turned triumphantly to Bruce.

"We've got it made, Bruce!" he exclaimed. "We get to stay at camp. Now, we can sneak off and find that gold mine!"

CHAPTER 7

THE SHADOW

Kent and Bruce worked very hard at camp during the next few days. They did all the extra work that was assigned to them without complaining. They memorized the Bible verses with the rest of the guys and were at every session on time. They both took part in a way they hadn't done since they arrived at camp. Bob noticed it and spoke to their counselor about it.

"You know, Tom," he said, "it looks as though Kent and Bruce are finally going to straighten out and join in on our camp program."

Tom agreed.

"Their attitude is better too," Bob went on. "I wrote to Danny and Kay last night and told them about it."

Tom leaned against a nearby tree. "If we could just write Danny and Kay that Kent had been saved, it would really thrill them. I can't quite understand him. There are times when he seems as though he's so close to making a decision that he'll do it within the next few minutes. Then again, he acts as though he'll never become a Christian."

"We'll have to keep praying for him."

Walt continued to testify to Kent at every opportunity.

"I can tell you this much, Kent, you don't know what living is until you've confessed your sin and put your trust in the Lord Jesus Christ."

Kent scowled at him. "Look who's talkin'."

"I thought I was having a big time when we were running around and getting into trouble, but I wasn't. I was half-scared all the time, or else I was in trouble with my parents for not minding. I was always being punished for something. You don't know what it is to be happy and have fun until you become a Christian."

Kent's lips curled. "When I want to be preached at, I'll let you know."

Although he was able to stop Walt from talking to him about Christ, Kent still had to listen when his former pal got up during testimony time and told what the Lord had done for him. When that happened, Kent squirmed miserably and fought against making a decision.

After several days of extra work detail and restricted privileges at camp there was a four-day horseback trip scheduled. Everyone in camp was talking about it. As soon as Kent could find Bruce the two of them went to Bob's cabin.

"It won't do any good for us to talk to him," Bruce protested, hanging back. "You heard what he said to us. He won't let us go."

"We'll never know until we ask him." The muscles in Kent's face tightened. "We've just got to get to go."

Bob was at his desk in the cabin when they entered. He looked up, smiling pleasantly. Kent shifted nervously from one foot to the other.

"We came to talk to you about the horseback trip," he said. "We know we don't deserve to go, but we sure would like to."

The director picked up a pencil and thoughtfully toyed with it. "I didn't put any time limit on the restrictions because I wanted to see how you would do." He paused, looking from one to the other. "And I'm happy to tell you that I think you've both been trying hard. If you wish to make the trail ride it's all right with me."

The boys were elated.

The following day the guys in the three cabins that were going to make the trip began getting everything ready. They assembled their food and gear besides attending all the Bible sessions. It kept them busy.

The following morning shortly after breakfast they mounted their horses and started up the narrow trail toward the top of the mountain. Bob led the way, and Tom brought up the rear.

The trail was beautiful. It crossed the creek several times and wound through the forest of aspen and evergreen. At noon they stopped on the banks of the mountain stream and built their fire.

There was quite a bit of work to do, but Kent managed to duck out of his share and slip out of the sight of the others to a place where he could unobtrusively scan the mountain. An icy numbness clamped its fingers about his stomach and squeezed it into a tight little knot. Everything looked alike. It was no wonder Doc Staughton had spent a whole lifetime searching for his grandfather's mine. Kent and Bruce could just as well have stayed in camp. They sure weren't going to be able to find anything. Kent was still standing there when Bob came up behind him.

"Looking for something special, Kent?" he asked quietly.

Startled, the boy turned.

"Oh no," he blurted. "No, I ain't lookin' for nothin' special."

"The rest of the guys are working," Bob reminded him.

Kent's cheeks colored as he turned and began to pick up dry wood for the fire.

All the rest of the day he kept watching as they made their way upward, but he saw nothing. That night he complained to Bruce about it.

"I'm beginning to wonder why we came on this stupid trip anyway," he said.

"I've been having a lot of fun."

A sneer twisted Kent's thin face.

"That's good," he said. "That's just dandy. I suppose

the next thing you'll be tellin' me is that you've gone off and got yourself saved, and you don't want to have nothin' to do with a guy like me."

Bruce wasn't saved at the campfire meeting that night, but somebody else was. Somebody who shook Kent almost as much as Bruce would have. It all began when Walt gave his testimony again. It seemed to Kent that he was always giving his testimony. When Walt finished, Bob gave a short message and an invitation.

Lee Nelson got to his feet and went forward. Kent stared after him.

"Would you look at that!" Anger flared in his eyes. For a moment he stood rigidly, then turned and stormed off into the darkness. "I'll show 'em!" he blurted. "I'll show 'em all!"

He stayed away from the campfire until after the service was over and the guys were heading for their sleeping bags. Then he crept back in silence and went to bed.

The following day was torture for Kent. Just looking at Lee was enough to send a hot flush of anger surging through his body. And he was furious to see Walt and Lee riding together.

"Look at 'em," he said to Bruce. "They think they're too good for the rest of us now that they're Christians."

Later, however, something happened that made Kent forget all about Lee and his decision. It was almost time for them to stop for the night when Kent saw a dark shadow almost completely hidden by brush a couple hundred yards off the trail. He reined up his horse sharply, and Bruce came up beside him.

"What's the matter? Do you see something?"

"I'll tell you about it later."

Carefully Kent got a bearing on the opening in the hill lining it up with a couple of landmarks so he could be sure and locate it again. Then he rode on. Tom, who was behind him, rode up to where he was.

"Is there something wrong, Kent?" he asked.

Kent looked surprised. "No, of course not. There's nothin' wrong."

"You stopped for a minute and I figured something was wrong."

"Oh that," Kent lied. "I thought I had a stirrup coming loose, so I stopped to check it. But it's all right."

They had not ridden more than half a mile further when Bob stopped them in a small clearing and set them to making camp. Everyone pitched in eagerly. Some of the guys put up the tents while others gathered wood and carried water. By the time the camp was ready the appointed cooks were getting supper.

Stealthily Kent got Bruce off to one side.

"Just as soon as we've finished eating, slip away and we'll meet down by the creek."

"What for?"

"We're going back to see if that opening I saw is really a mine or only a cave."

Bruce shook his head. "Nothing doing. Look at the mess we got into the last time we sneaked off."

"Bob hasn't told us we can't leave this camp."

There was a short hesitation.

"I guess not."

"Besides, he'll never notice that we're gone. We'll only be away twenty minutes or so." Excitement kindled flames in Kent's eyes.

"Are you sure we're only going to be gone twenty minutes?" Bruce asked.

"I'll guarantee it."

"OK. But I'm coming back in twenty minutes."

They started away, but Kent turned back. "We'd better take flashlights and a piece of rope if we've got them."

"I don't have a rope. And I don't think I've even got any fresh batteries for my flashlight. I meant to get some before we left camp, but I forgot."

Kent scowled his displeasure.

"OK, OK. I've got my own flashlight and we can get along without a rope."

CHAPTER 8

KENT'S DISCOVERY

Kent moved stealthily back to his tent as casually as though he was going to put his camera away. Once inside, he got his flashlight and scooted around back and into the trees. He moved so quietly that nobody saw him. Bruce was there waiting for him.

It didn't take them long to reach the spot where Kent had been when he first saw the opening. He stopped and pointed to it.

"It's right over there."

Disappointment clouded Bruce's voice. "That doesn't look like a mine to me. It looks more like a cave."

"Yeh, but remember what old Doc Staughton said about that? He said sometimes you can't tell the difference until you get inside and take a good, close look." Kent started toward the opening. "Let's get goin'. We can't tell nothin' about it from here."

Bruce hurried to catch up with him.

"If you saw it from the trail, how do you figure it's going to be a secret from anybody else? That trail's used a lot. A hundred people could've seen it before you did."

"Maybe. And maybe not. The sun was shining on it just right to make the dark of the opening stand out. I don't think I'd have seen it at all if we hadn't been along at just the right time."

They walked directly over to the opening and for a moment or two looked around with growing excitement.

"We still don't know whether it's a mine or a cave," Bruce said.

"No, but we'll find out. All we've got to do is go inside a little way."

Bruce looked at his watch. "We don't have time, Kent."

"It'll only take five minutes."

"You can go in there if you want to, but I'm going back. I'm not getting in any more trouble with Mr. Anders."

Kent snorted. "Bob Anders doesn't scare me." He took a step or two inside the opening. "It's only going to take a sec to find out whether this is a cave or a mine."

"Well...," Bruce said reluctantly.

Kent Gilbert took that for agreement and advanced slowly into the darkness of the opening. He switched on his flashlight to illuminate the narrow passageway. Bruce was right behind him.

"If this is a mine," he said, "I've got a hunch it's the right one."

"Suppose we do find the gold?" Bruce asked. "Who would it belong to? Doc?"

Kent bristled. "Why would it belong to him? He isn't the one who found it."

Bruce did not reply.

"We've got to go in a little further," Kent said. "We sure can't tell anything from here."

Bruce shrank back.

"Do you think we should?"

For answer Kent kept moving, and Bruce followed with growing reluctance.

* * *

Back at the overnight camp the guys had finished doing the dishes and were policing the campgrounds. The detail that had been assigned to carry wood for the campfire service had the fire ready to light.

It was only then that Bob missed Kent and Bruce. He went over to where Lee was standing and asked about them.

"I saw them quite a while ago," Lee said. "They were together down by the creek."

Bob glanced at his watch. If it had been anyone other than those two, he would not have been concerned at all. But with a guy like Kent Gilbert, one could never tell. He decided to wait for another ten minutes.

When ten minutes had passed with no sign of the boys, Bob sought out Tom and talked with him about it.

"Tom, I'd like to have you take charge here," he concluded. "You and the other counselors can start the campfire service."

Tom looked questioningly at him.

"I'm going to take Walt and Lee and see if we can find those two characters," he said. "I guess we quit punishing them too soon. Apparently, they haven't learned that they've got to do what we ask them to."

"Are you sure you won't need me?" Tom asked.

"I'd like to have you, but I think you're needed more right here at camp. We'll probably find that they're just goofing off along the creek somewhere."

Bob led Walt and Lee out of the camp and down along the narrow, winding mountain stream. In a moment or two he picked up the boys' footprints.

"They went this way," he said.

For more than a quarter of a mile their footprints were quite easy to follow. Then they disappeared completely.

"Why don't you guys go on ahead and see if you can pick them up? I'll look around here."

There was a long, narrow rocky ledge. Beyond it and on either side the ground was as hard as concrete. At last Walt and Lee came back to the place where Bob was looking.

"Not a sign of them," Lee said.

"It doesn't look as though we're going to be able to pick up their tracks either."

"Where do you suppose they are?" Walt asked. For the first time there was concern in his voice.

* * *

Kent and Bruce were moving slowly along the dark passageway guided by the faint yellow beam of Kent's flashlight. Bruce noticed that the beam was weak. Almost as weak as his own light had been.

"That flashlight sure doesn't seem to be very strong," he said. "Don't you think we should go back now?"

"We will," Kent retorted, "in a couple of minutes."

"But you promised."

Anger flickered in Kent's eyes. "I said we'd go back as soon as we find out what we want to know."

"We saw the toolmarks at the opening," Bruce countered. "We're pretty sure it's a mine."

"Sure." Contempt thinly edged Kent's voice. "We *thought* we saw some toolmarks, but we aren't sure we did. And we won't be sure until we see some timber bracing."

There was a brief silence.

"If you're not going back, you're going to have to stay here alone," Bruce declared. "I'm going to get back to camp before we get into some real trouble."

Kent's hand snaked out quickly and grasped Bruce by the forearm. "Don't be stupid!" he rasped. "I just want to go another dozen yards or so to see if we can find anything. Then I'll leave with you."

"All right," Bruce agreed reluctantly. "But if you don't come back with me, then I'm going alone."

A little further on they came to some timbers that lined the tunnel to give support to the ceiling.

"Look!" Kent's voice shook with excitement. "I told you that we'd find something if we just came a little further. Now we know for sure that we're in a mine."

He flashed the light around picking out a rusted hammer, a pick, and some other tools with the faint beam.

"What's this?" he asked, going over and kneeling to examine them. "Somebody was working this mine and just went off and left the stuff here."

"Do you suppose it belongs to old Doc's grandfather?"

"Who else?"

Kent continued to look over the tools. Behind them was a small box that held something that looked like rifle cartridge brass.

"What's that?" Bruce wondered.

"I don't know for sure, but I think they must be dynamite caps."

"If that's what they are you'd better leave them right where you found them," Bruce said. "They're apt to blow up."

Kent took a small handful and shoved them into his pocket.

"They're not going to blow up if a guy's careful with 'em."

As he straightened, his flashlight beam caught a glitter of light on the tunnel wall.

"Bruce!" he cried, his voice shaking.

"What's the matter?" His excitement fired Bruce with excitement too.

"Something in the wall is shining!"

Bruce stared numbly at the flicker of light on the dark stone wall.

"Gold!"

With that he took his jackknife from his pocket and tried to dig one of the rocks from the wall with the leather punch. Kent snatched up the old pick.

"Here," he exclaimed, "this'll be easier."

"I–I think I'm gettin' it!" Even as he spoke, he was able to flake off a couple of pieces the size of golf balls or a little smaller.

"Let me at it with this!" Kent cried. "I can get it in a hurry!"

CHAPTER 9

CAVE-IN

Bob Anders took a deep breath and stared numbly about the mountainside. Already the sun was setting and the shadows on the steep slope were long and foreboding. Trees blurred together and rocks took on strange, unnatural shapes. It wouldn't be long until darkness fell. And still they had found no sign of Kent and Bruce. Lee, who had just accepted Christ as his Savior the night before, turned to Bob.

"This could be Kent's idea of a good joke," he said. "He and Bruce might be hiding in the brush somewhere right now watching us and laughing because we can't pick up their trail."

Bob studied the tracks that ended so abruptly.

"These tracks look to me as though they were heading somewhere in particular. I think they just happened to get up on this granite outcrop and hard clay that doesn't leave any footprints."

The boys stared helplessly at him.

"What're we going to do?" Walt urged.

"The only thing we can do is go back to camp and get a search party organized," Bob answered. "There's no telling where a couple of guys like those two would go or what they'd try to do."

"Are there enough guys up here to make a search party?" Lee asked.

"I'll have to ride back to the Bible camp," Bob explained. "The forest ranger lives close by. He'll put out a call and get some men to come up and help look for them."

Lee winced. "Is it *that* dangerous?"

Bob nodded cryptically.

A few minutes later he saddled his horse and started down the narrow, twisting trail. It was going to be a long, slow ride in the dark.

* * *

Kent and Bruce had momentarily forgotten Bob and the fact that he might be looking for them. They had forgotten everything except the sparkling ore they were prying out of the tunnel wall. It wasn't long until they had their pockets full.

"Wish we had a couple of sacks along, don't you?"

Bruce laughed nervously. "Maybe we could get one of the pack horses down here and take out a whole load of gold."

"We ain't got a thing to worry about," Kent said, "as long as we keep our mouths shut. Nobody else knows anything about this but us. We can come back here and get a whole train load if we want to." He grinned impulsively. "Now, aren't you glad you stayed with me?"

A moment or two later they hurried back in the direction they had come. They hadn't gone far when they came to a place where several tunnels met. Kent stopped uncertainly and surveyed the little chamber with his flashlight.

"Which way did we come in here, Bruce?"

"I don't know." Fear gleamed in Bruce's eyes.

Kent laughed with exaggerated carelessness as though to show Bruce he was not really as scared as he'd ever been in his life.

"We're goin' to get out of here before old Bob has himself a heart attack," he said. "Come on."

He wasn't at all sure which tunnel would lead them back to the mine entrance, but he didn't let Bruce know that. Confidently he chose one and started off. As the minutes passed, a nagging uncertainty began to chill him. Grimly he fought it off.

They hadn't gone far when his flashlight flickered and went off.

"Kent!" Bruce cried in terror. "Turn your light on!"

"I–I can't!" For the first time Kent's fear was stark and unhidden.

* * *

The ride back to the camp at the foot of the mountain was a long one for Bob, but he pushed his weary mount as hard as he dared. It was daylight when he rode into the grounds. One of the counselors who was just getting up saw him and came running out to him.

"Bob!" he cried. "What's wrong?"

Weariness stole the life from Bob's voice – weariness and concern.

"We've got a couple of kids lost on the mountain," he blurted. "Get Harrison on the phone, will you? Tell him about it so he can get some men lined up to help look for them."

Without asking any more questions the counselor ran for the telephone. Peggy Anders saw him dash past her window and went to the door to look out.

"Bob!" She scurried out to him.

Hurriedly he related what had happened.

"It's bad, isn't it?" she asked simply when he had finished.

Bob nodded. "It's worse than that, if possible. It's wild, dangerous country for a couple of kids who aren't used to the mountains." He went into the house with her and sat down wearily.

"What are you going to do?"

"I think I'll go up and get old Doc Staughton for one thing. Nobody else knows the hills better than he does."

* * *

Back in the mine Kent and Bruce faced their new crisis with growing hysteria. For a long, agonizing minute neither spoke. When Bruce did, his voice quavered.

"Are–are you sure you can't get the flashlight to go on?" he asked almost hopefully.

"Of course I'm sure!" Kent's temper exploded. "Don't you think I c'n keep a flashlight burning?"

"I wouldn't know," the other boy retorted hotly. "You sure have fouled things up so far."

"Look who's talkin'! If I'd known you were such a baby, I'd have left you home!"

"Believe me, I wish I'd stayed at camp."

"Nobody made you come!"

Bruce was on the verge of tears. "If we'd done like I wanted to, we wouldn't be in a jam like this."

"If we'd done like you wanted to, we'd never have found this mine in the first place." Contempt curled Kent's thin lips. "You'd have been so scared of your own shadow that we'd have been sittin' back at camp listenin' to those guys preach at us, 'stead of bein' down here with our pockets full of gold!"

Bruce was not to be stilled however.

"We should've gone back to camp after we found this was a mine. We should've gone back and talked to Mr. Anders. We should've gotten him to come along and help us explore the mine. But no! You had to keep begging me to go just a little farther with you until–"

"Aw, shut up!"

Kent put both hands on Bruce's chest and gave

him a hard shove. He fell backward. His shoulder hit against the timbers that had been put in to shore up the tunnel when the mine was being worked regularly.

There was an ominous cracking noise.

Kent froze!

"Wh-wh-what was that?" he cried out.

Bruce struggled to regain his feet. Even as he did so the timbers cracked and rumbled.

"Look out!"

The timbers, rotten and weak from long years of use, broke without further warning. Rocks and dirt came tumbling down with a terrifying roar!

* * *

Bob Anders did not even want to stay in camp long enough to have breakfast.

"I don't have time to eat, Peggy," he told his wife. "I'm going to have the boys saddle a fresh horse for me so I can ride up to Doc Staughton's."

"You've got to have breakfast, Bob. You've ridden all night, and the chances are you'll have to ride all the way back to the campsite before you get another chance to eat."

"Those boys are lost up there, Peggy," he said with fear edging his voice. "Don't you understand?"

"I'm as concerned about them as you are, Bob," she countered. "But I'm concerned about you too." She moved toward the stove. "I'll have breakfast for you in less than ten minutes."

Bob didn't realize how hungry he was until he started to eat. He was just finishing when Gene Hall, the assistant director of the camp, came over.

"Everything's all lined up, Bob. I talked with Harrison a minute ago. He put out a general alarm and will have forty or fifty men ready to go up and look for the boys within an hour."

Bob smiled briefly, but the anxiety did not leave his face.

"Fine. And thanks, Gene. I was just going to phone Harrison and see what he planned on doing."

"Anything else you want me to take care of?"

"Nothing special, thanks. I'll go up and help with the search in any way I can. You see that things continue here."

"The guys all know about Bruce and Kent by now," Gene said. "It's going to be hard to keep a regular program going."

"I know that but do the best you can." Bob got his heavy jacket, for he knew it could be cold up on the mountain at night. Then he went out to mount his fresh saddle horse.

The ride up to Doc Staughton's was a short one. And he reached the old prospector's place just in time. Doc was about ready to go out on one of his prospecting jaunts when Bob rode up.

"Sure, I'll go with you." Doc's expression changed. "To tell you the truth, Bob, I feel sorta responsible for them two kids runnin' off that way."

"How could you be responsible for that?"

"Well, you see, they was up here to see me one day not too long ago."

"Yes, I know," Bob answered. "We had to punish them for leaving camp without permission."

"Well, when they was here I got to tellin' 'em stories about the old mines hereabouts. They was sure powerful interested." He took a long breath. "The more I think 'bout it the more sure I am they got some wild notion 'bout sneakin' off an' findin' my grandpappy's mine. It makes me feel plumb responsible."

"You shouldn't feel that way, Doc. You don't know these two boys. They've been real troublemakers ever since they came to camp. It wasn't your fault they ran away." Bob paused thoughtfully. "I suppose we made a mistake in even taking them."

The grizzled old prospector shook his head.

"Now, Bob, don't you go to talkin' that way," he said. "You don't ever make no mistake when you try to help someone." He turned back to his cabin. "I'll git me a jacket an' hat an' be right with you."

Bob waited impatiently. It only took Doc a couple of minutes to get his things. Nevertheless, Bob was concerned about the delay and anxious to get back to the camp.

He knew all too well what the country the boys were lost in was like. He knew the kind of danger a couple of headstrong city boys could get themselves into. All too often even a man who was used to the mountains would get into real trouble through no fault of his own.

Bob shivered apprehensively.

CHAPTER 10

THE SEARCH

As the rocks and dirt tumbled to block the tunnel, Kent and Bruce leaped away. Dust billowed about them in great, choking clouds. Not until it began to settle did either of the boys speak.

"Bruce?" Fear was evident in Kent's voice.

There was no answer.

"Bruce?" he demanded fearfully. "Are you hurt?"

"I–I don't think so." There was a short silence. "Are you?"

"I don't think so either."

For a brief, agonizing minute neither said anything. When Bruce did speak his voice was all but hysterical.

"Kent!" he shouted. "I can't move my leg! I can't move my leg!"

Kent crawled through the darkness back to him. Although he could not see Bruce, he felt around until he found him.

"I can't move my leg," Bruce murmured.

"Try again," Kent ordered.

"It's no use. I can't do it!" Fear choked his voice. "There's something on it, I tell you. I'm trapped. I'm trapped!"

"M-m-maybe I can help you."

Kent groped desperately for his flashlight hoping to be able to *get* it to work again, but it was gone.

"Why don't you try to get your flashlight to working again?" Bruce asked.

"I–I can't!"

Kent Gilbert found his companion's trapped leg and felt along it until he came to the obstruction that pinned the frightened boy to the floor of the tunnel. His hands examined it quickly. A piece of the timber and some stone and dirt had caught Bruce and held him there. Grimly Kent started to work.

"Do–do you think you can get me out?"

"I think so." He was panting heavily. "When I lift this timber, pull your leg out."

Bracing his feet, Kent lifted with all the strength his frail young body could muster. At last, he was able to lift the heavy timber a scant inch.

"Now!" The words hissed out. "Pull your leg free, Bruce!"

Already the boy was jerking to get his leg from under the heavy timber.

"I–I–can't–hold–it–much–longer!"

"I'm out!" Exultation and gratitude filled Bruce's voice. "I'm free!"

Kent sank back on the pile of rubble, exhausted by the effort. It was several moments before he could speak.

"Do–do you think you're all right?"

Bruce moved his foot speculatively. "It still aches some," he said, "but I–I don't think any bones are broken."

"That's a good thing."

For a moment all was quiet.

"Kent?" Bruce said weakly.

"Yeh." Kent's voice snarled his irritation. "What do you want now?"

"How long do you s'pose it'll be before Bob and the others find us down here?"

Kent swallowed hard. "How should I know?" he demanded. "I'm not a fortune-teller."

"They–they don't even know where we are."

"You ain't tellin' me nothin' new," Kent retorted.

A dry sob escaped Bruce's lips. "You know, we're in a terrible spot."

The silence was deafening.

"We ain't licked yet!"

Bruce sat up and rubbed his ankle speculatively.

"We won't find our way out of here!" A sob broke his trembling voice. "I just know we won't!"

* * *

Bob Anders and Doc Staughton made their way up the mountainside. By the time they got to the camp, the forest ranger and a number of ranchers had arrived. More were riding in. Harrison, who had been talking to the men and boys assembled there, stopped as Bob and Doc rode up.

"I was just organizing the search," he explained. "I'd like to have those of you who know the mountains well step forward."

Several men stepped forward and Harrison put them in charge of small groups. At last, everything was ready for Harrison to send out search parties. Only then did Bob step forward and speak.

"Before you men go, I'd like to have a word of prayer."

The men and boys bowed their heads, and Bob prayed for their safety and for the success of the search. The prayer seemed to make everybody feel better, even those who were not Christians.

* * *

Kent stood in silence in the mine tunnel, both hands touching the wall.

"Bruce," he said, "we can feel our way along. We'll figure out how to get out of this old mine yet."

"How can we?" Bruce demanded. He was near hysteria. "The entrance is sealed off, and a mine's only got one entrance!"

"Maybe. Maybe not!"

"And, even if there is another way out of the mine, we're not going to be able to find it without a flashlight."

"We can try!" Kent almost screamed at him. "It's better than sittin' here."

Bruce and Kent continued to move tensely along the tunnel, feeling the wall with their hands. After several minutes, Bruce paused.

"Kent?"

"What do you want now?"

"Have–have you ever prayed?"

"Now, don't start that stuff!" Kent snorted derisively. "You sound like Walt and Lee!"

There was a slight hesitation.

"You know, Kent," he continued, "if we'd done what Lee did last night at the campfire service, we– we wouldn't be in this jam!"

There was no answer.

"I don't know about you, but I wish *I* had!"

"You wish you'd done what?" Bitterness made the words ugly and distasteful.

"I wish I'd become a Christian when Lee did," Bruce said. "At least I–I wouldn't have to worry about what'd happen to me if we don't –I mean, if I don't–" He could not finish what he was saying.

"Hurry up!" his companion broke in. "And forget that kind of talk! We've got to keep movin' if we're goin' to make it outa here before dark!"

But Bruce had made up his mind.

"Bob Anders said a guy didn't have to go forward <u>in</u> a meeting in order to get saved," he went on. "I'm going to become a Christian right now."

With that, he knelt right where they were.

While Kent stood there listening in disgust, Bruce poured out his heart to God.

"I've done a lot of things I shouldn't have done," he began. "I know that. I've disobeyed my parents and–and been in trouble at school and–and with the law. I've been so bad I–I don't even know why You would want to save me."

Kent squirmed uncomfortably. He had done all those things too. Only more so than Bruce. He'd been in trouble with just about everybody.

"But Mr. Anders read to us from the Bible that You loved us so much that You sent Your only Son to die on the cross so we could be saved." There was a brief hesitation. "I–I don't know what I'm supposed to do now except to just ask You to save me. I didn't pay close enough attention when Mr. Anders was talking, but if–if I'm supposed to do something else, You show me what it is and–and I'll do it. I sure am sick of trying to run my own life and getting into one mess like this after another. *1 want to be a Christian!*"

Kent didn't know whether Bruce was bawling when he prayed or not, but he supposed he was. It would be just about like him. Kent didn't know what was the matter with everybody anyway. Why did they have to let this religious business get hold of them? He gulped and scrubbed at his own eyes with the back of a grimy fist.

For an instant he fought against an almost uncontrollable desire to do the same as Bruce had done.

But in desperation he checked himself. They could just forget that bit, as far as he was concerned. They weren't going to hook him with it.

When Bruce first began to pray, his voice had been on the verge of hysteria, but as he prayed, he began to quiet down. When he finished, he was completely calm.

"Well, are you done now?" Kent demanded, contempt coloring every word he spoke.

Bruce did not answer him directly.

"Kent," he began, getting slowly to his feet. "I don't know whether you've thought much about this or not, but we're in real trouble. We–we may never get out of here."

Kent swallowed hard. "Now what kind of talk is that?"

"I'm just facing facts. The tunnel's blocked and we can't get back to the entrance, at least not the way we came in. And nobody knows where we are. They may have to search this mountain for a month before they find this old mine or think of looking in it."

Fear filled Kent's voice. "What're you tryin' to do? Scare me?"

"I'm just trying to get you to see what trouble we're in so–so you'll see how important it is for you to do what I did just now."

"Hmph!" Kent snorted contemptuously.

"If we didn't get out of here, you'd want to go to heaven, wouldn't you?"

Noisily Kent drew in a long breath.

"When're you goin' to stop preachin' at me?"

"I used to fight against giving my heart to God," Bruce said, "just the way you're doing now, but it's like Walt said the other night. There's no reason why we have to go on living our lives in our own strength and making such a mess of things. We can let Jesus help us, especially when we're in a spot like we're in right now."

Kent gritted his teeth. What Bruce said was true. Ever since he could remember he'd been trying to run his life exactly the way he wanted to. And all he'd ever done was get into trouble and hurt the people who had been good to him. People like Danny and Kay Orlis, Bob Anders, and Tom Channing.

Lee hadn't been a Christian long enough for Kent to see how he was going to make out, but Walt sure seemed to be different. Not that he was perfect or anything like that. Tom still had to get after him every once in a while for making a noise after lights out. And he still did other things that even Kent knew better than to do. But his attitude was different. He didn't get mad when he was called down, and he really tried to live the way he knew he should.

Another thing that surprised Kent was that Walt seemed to have as much fun as he ever did. He laughed and kidded a lot – maybe even more than he had before. There was no doubt about it. Walt wasn't the same guy. He was building a good reputation; he was happier and more relaxed than he had ever been. Kent longed for the same change in his own life. For a brief instant the pull to yield to Christ was all but overwhelming. Yet Kent continued to hold out.

Even now he couldn't turn his life over to Christ or to anyone. He was going to try to work things out on his own for a little while longer and see how it went. At some time – if they ever got out of this mess, after he'd had a chance to do things his own way for a while – he was going to become a Christian.

"This is rough right now, Bruce," he said, trying to laugh a little as he changed the subject. "But when we get out of here and show everybody our gold, we'll be glad we came down here and found it."

Kent stopped momentarily and wiped the sweat from his forehead with a trembling hand. They had already been in the mine for hours and hours, and no one knew where they were. What would they do if they didn't find a way out before long?

Fear welled unquenchably within him, and the ache in his heart continued to grow.

* * *

At the overnight camp where the men had set up a base of operations for the search, Doc Staughton sought out Tom Channing.

"Hello there, young guy," he said pleasantly.

"Hi." He had liked the grizzled old prospector since the first time they met.

"You goin' out with anyone in particular."

"Not that I know of," Tom said. "I was just going to ask Bob what he wanted me to do."

Doc looked him over appraisingly.

"You c'n save your breath," he said. "You're a-goin' with me."

"Fine. Who else'll be in the party?"

"This ain't no party. We're goin' out to look for them kids – just you 'n' me."

"Won't there be anyone else along?" Tom asked.

"Nope." Doc shook his head emphatically. "They'd just be in the way." He took a deep breath. "I've got me a little theory about them kids. I've jest been a-settin' here tryin' to figger it out. I don't reckon on goin' traipsin' over the whole mountain to find them boys."

Tom listened with growing interest.

"Them boys was powerful concerned about that mine of my grandpappy's," Doc continued. "I've got me a hunch that they thought they could find it on their own."

"And you think maybe they did?" he asked. "Is that it?"

The old man laughed shortly.

"Now that'd be somethin', wouldn't it? I've been a-goin' up an' down these here mountains fer most of fifty years an' ain't found nothin' yet. 'Twould sure be a good one iffen they'd go out and find it right off, now wouldn't it?"

The two of them left the camp and walked briskly down to the stream.

"Bob said they followed the boys' tracks almost a quarter of a mile down the mountain. That'll give us some sort of a start."

Doc Staughton nodded. "We can go thataway and look first," he said, "iffen that's what you'd like, but I still figger on goin' to all the mines around these here parts that I know about. I jest figger that's where they disappeared to."

"Your idea's better than mine," Tom said. "You take the lead. I'll be right behind you."

Doc led him to two mines in the immediate vicinity. He looked expertly about the opening of each before shaking his head.

"Nope. They ain't been here. Neither one of 'em."

Tom Channing had difficulty in hiding his disappointment.

As they approached the third mine, however, Doc's sharp old eyes picked out a broken twig.

"Now, sonny," he said, "lookie here. Somebody's been this way not too long ago." He indicated the break. "Not more'n a day ago, I'd say."

Tom's eyes brightened. "Do you think it was Kent and Bruce?"

The old man eyed him with quiet amusement.

"Now, I can't rightly say as to that, seein' as how they didn't leave no callin' card."

At the mouth of the mine, however, they found something more. Tom saw it at almost the same time Doc did.

"Look!" He ran forward and knelt to stare at two sets of footprints in the soft dirt.

Doc Staughton nodded. "Yes sirree. It looks's though we've finally found somethin'."

"It could be them, don't you think?"

"I reckon it could be. The fact is, I figger it was. The way them boys was talkin' I just knew they was goin' to head for one of the old mines 'round these parts."

Tom swallowed hard. "But where do you think they are now?"

"I reckon the best place to look is right inside."

CHAPTER 11

THE SANDSTONE CLUE

Old Doc Staughton started into the mine with Tom close behind.

"They would have had to pick this one," Doc retorted almost to himself.

"Why? Is this mine worse than any of the others?" Doc frowned.

"I wouldn't rightly say she was any worse than the others. All of these here old mines is mighty dangerous. None of 'em is fittin' fer a couple of greenhorn kids to be nosin' around in. There's a hundred things that could happen to 'em. And this here mine's bigger 'n both of them others put t'gether."

From somewhere in the pocket of his jacket, Doc pulled out his flashlight and switched it on. Its powerful beam searched the tunnel ahead.

"How come you carry a flashlight, Doc?"

The old man laughed drily.

"Listen, sonny, I always bring 'long the things I need. You forgit I've been a-pokin' 'round in these here mines most of my life. And one of the first things I learned was to carry a good flashlight and some spare batteries with me all the time." Doc sighed. "There jest ain't nothin' darker'n a mine!"

The two of them walked slowly into the big mine. The old prospector's flashlight covered each foot of the way before they moved on, examining each section of the tunnel ceiling and each timber that held it up. For a minute or two they walked in silence.

"See any signs that they've been here?" Tom asked at last.

Doc's lower lip firmed.

"Not exactly. Only this's the main tunnel and I jest figger maybe they kept on goin' down it."

"There's something that bothers me about all this, Doc," Tom said.

"What's that, sonny?"

"If they're in here – and I'm like you; I've got a good hunch they are – how come they haven't come back out yet?"

"That's what's set me to thinkin'. Unless they went and got themselves lost or trapped or snakebit or somethin' like that."

Tom shivered.

They walked on slowly for several yards when the powerful flashlight beam picked up the debris that blocked the mine tunnel.

"Doc!" Tom's shrill cry echoed and reechoed through the mine.

The flashlight in Doc's hand began to quiver.

"A cave-in!"

"And as far as I can tell, it's a fresh un!"

Suddenly Tom felt as though there was no longer any strength left in his young body. His knees sagged and sweat beaded his forehead. He tried to speak, but there were no words. Instead, he moved forward mechanically and threw a stone from the pile. That seemed to loose the bonds that had been holding him motionless. He began to claw frantically at the rocks and timbers until Doc stopped him.

"Ain't no use in that, sonny." Doc's voice was gentle. "I've seen a heap of these cave-ins in my day. Can't get it cleared out that way!"

Tom raised his head, and for an instant his temper raged within him.

"We can't know for sure until we try!"

"There's just no way you an' me can git that opened up, sonny, much as we want to. There's tons and tons of rock jammed in there. It's goin' to take a sight of help to make a dent in that. We've got to have help and plenty of it."

"Why don't you go get Bob and the others?" Tom demanded quickly. "I'll stay here and do what I can."

But Doc shook his head.

"You c'n go faster'n me, Tom. You skin out of here and get everybody over here as quick as you can."

Tom started away on the run.

For a long while after he was gone Doc stood there, staring down at the debris that blocked the tunnel. His breath was coming in short, quick gasps and his whole being trembled. Those boys were trapped somewhere on the other side of that huge pile of rocks, dirt, and timbers. And, like as not, they were panic-stricken.

He should never have told them about his grandfather's mine. That was what had caused all the trouble.

For something to do, Doc walked slowly to the mine entrance and stepped out into the fresh air, breathing deeply. The breeze cooled him as it began to dry the perspiration that dampened his clothes. He took a few steps to the right and glanced up the mountain. Tom should be coming back with the others at any time now. And when they got there, they would get to work on the cave-in. In a little while they'd be able to find out how bad it was.

He straightened slowly.

He had known cave-ins that were almost impossible to clear. He had known others that caught unsuspecting men beneath them and, miserably, he turned the other way.

For several minutes Doc stared blankly out into space.

What was the matter with that young guy who had gone for help? He should've been back long ago. Doc looked at his watch and grinned sheepishly. Tom had scarcely had time to get to the camp, let alone to get the men together and lead them back to the mine.

But with those kids trapped inside somewhere, each minute seemed like an hour. They could panic in a situation like this. And if they did, there was no knowing what they would do!

Doc walked slowly down the mountain slope a hundred yards or so and to the left about the same distance. His plan was to get to a place where he could see the trail so he could know when help was coming. A little farther to the left and he would be able to see the campsite. He was moving over when his eye caught a little clump of brush not far away.

What it was that attracted him he wasn't sure. It looked very much like any other clump of brush that stood against the mountainside. He would probably have ignored it except that long years of searching the mountains almost foot by foot made him curious and gave him a sort of sixth sense about the natural order of things. He turned his attention to the clump of brush, mumbling to himself.

"I don't know why I'm comin' over here this way. I must be gettin' old 'n' childish thinkin' I have to take a close look at everything I see. There's nothin' here but a clump of brush an'–." He checked himself suddenly.

There was something queer about that clump of brush. Doc realized now that it was the dark shadow behind it. The brush had grown in such a way as to hide a small opening in the side of the hill. That in itself was strange enough. It was almost as though someone had planted it there to hide the opening.

A guy could have ridden within five feet of it and have never seen it. That was probably the reason he had never found it before. Surely he had been on the mountain often enough to have passed it a dozen times.

Doc moved over to the hole in the ground and studied it intently. It was small. Just large enough for a man to wriggle through, and much too small for the entrance to a mine. Or was it?

A clever prospector who figured he might have to get out in a hurry and didn't want anyone else to find it might have made a small entrance. And he might have planted a clump of brush in front to hide it from view. That would make the mine, if indeed it was a mine, older than the state of Colorado. After organized government came into being, laws had been set up and a man's rights to his claim were recognized. He only had to register it. He didn't have to hide it. So it wasn't at all likely that this was even a mine. The fact that the opening was symmetrical was probably one of those freaks of nature that just happened.

Doc Staughton scratched his head and reasoned with himself. It had to be a cave. That's all there was to it. Still, that explanation didn't entirely satisfy him. Painfully he stooped and began to examine the ground around the opening.

It was then that he saw a corner of a flat stone partially embedded in the dirt just below the opening. It was a sort of sandstone, and the outcrop nearby was granite. That wasn't a freak of nature. That was sure. Somebody had carried it there.

Frantically Doc dug the packed dirt with his pocketknife. By this time, his pulse was racing, and his hands were trembling so much he could scarcely work.

At last, he had the dirt scraped off the piece of sandstone and rubbed it clean. There it was! The thing he had been looking for!

G. S.

The letters were crudely formed in the soft stone, but they were there – unmistakably – his grandfather's initials!

He had found the long-lost gold mine he had been looking for most of his life!

Doc Staughton began to tremble violently.

CHAPTER 12

HIDDEN SHAFT

In the mine Kent put aside his fears and summoned his strength once more.

"Ready to go again, Bruce?" he asked.

"As ready as you are."

They continued to move forward slowly, feeling their way along the edge of the tunnel. After what seemed to be an hour or two, they reached a sharp corner. Kent stopped, and Bruce bumped into him.

"Bruce!" he cried, "do you see anything?"

Bruce started to speak, but his mouth sagged open.

"A light!" Kent cried triumphantly.

There was a moment of silence.

"I told you we weren't whipped yet. There's a way out of this mine."

Sure enough! There was a beam of light at the far end of the tunnel. It was only a faint shaft of light, that was true. So faint that it did but little to dispel the darkness. But it was there nevertheless, like a lighthouse beam on a stormy night.

"God did answer my prayer." Bruce's thin voice broke. "I knew He would!"

"Come on!" Kent broke into a run, stumbled, and almost went sprawling. He caught himself and hurried on.

Once or twice, he started to speak, but he could not.

In a couple of minutes, they were directly beneath the small opening in the ceiling some ten or fifteen feet above the floor where they were standing. Kent could scarcely conceal his disappointment.

"It's not an entrance to the mine at all!" he said in dismay.

"It's an air shaft," Bruce explained. "They have to put them in big mines every so often so the men can get air down to the place where they're working."

"I know all that," Kent said gruffly. "I talked to old Doc Staughton too. But a lot of good it's going to do us." His voice grew hysterical. "It's just enough of an opening to tantalize us but not enough to do us any good."

Bruce thought for a moment.

"I don't know whether it would work or not," he pondered, "but I think maybe we can squeeze through that opening if we can climb up there."

"If we can climb up there," Kent echoed, belligerence mingling with the despair in his voice. "And just how are we goin' to manage that?"

Bruce moved forward, and in the faint light that drifted down to the bottom of the shaft, he began to examine the tunnel wall.

"We should be able to make some hand- and foot-holds to use in climbing, even in this rock," he said, more to himself than to his companion.

By this time Kent began to see there was a possibility of getting out. He moved to the opposite wall and began to look for some way up. Bruce found a place that seemed to offer the best possibilities. The wall was already rough and interspersed with a soft substance that was a little harder than clay. Taking out his scout knife with the leather punch, Bruce began to dig a foothold.

"Here," Kent said, "let me help."

With frantic haste the boys set to work, digging hand- and foot-holds in the wall of the tunnel. Kent worked faster than Bruce and started to climb first. Bruce waited and came up behind him.

As they went higher there were a few natural hand-holds. Kent sought them out with his fingers. Even then the going was very slow. But at last, he was within a short distance of the opening.

"There!" Relief was evident in his voice. "I think I can get through all right!"

He started to raise himself, but his blood froze in horror.

There was an ominous rattling sound near his head, and two beady eyes stared hatefully at him.

A rattlesnake!

It was coiled on the ledge just inside the airshaft opening.

The snake rattled again. Kent screamed and let go of the handhold, dropping to the floor of the mine shaft.

Bruce, who was clinging precariously to the wall just below where Kent had been, looked down. "Kent!" he called out. "Are you alright?"

"I'm all right," Kent quavered, "but you'd better get out of there! Th-the–that snake almost got me. You'll never be able to get by him!"

Still Bruce did not move.

"Don't try it, Bruce! It'll get you for sure!"

Bruce spoke with a calmness that surprised even him.

"Not if I can help it."

"There's nothing you c'n do up there," Kent persisted. "If you get any closer, the snake'll strike! Come on down!"

"There's nothing we can do from down there," Bruce said. "We've got to get that snake out of the way before we can do anything more about getting out of here."

Kent's voice broke.

"I–I think I'd rather stay in here than to b-brave that snake."

But Bruce was not listening to him. He took his knife from his pocket, found a chink in the rock, and began to work with the blade.

"Oh!" Disappointment tinged his voice.

"What's the matter?" Kent asked. "What'd you do?"

"I broke my knife."

"You'd better get down before you get into real trouble."

Bruce was working at the rock in the wall with his fingers.

"There!" he said at last. "I've got it!"

"What're you going to do?"

Bruce did not answer him. For an instant he weighed the rock in his hand, then prayed silently for strength and guidance. Kent stared up at him in amazement as Bruce began to inch forward holding the rock in his hand. He had moved close enough so the snake sensed his presence. It rattled suddenly.

Bruce froze where he was. Cold sweat moistened the back of his neck and ran down his forehead. His hands trembled ever so slightly. But he couldn't stop now. He had to go on!

Cautiously he raised himself until he could make out the big rattlesnake coiled just inside the air shaft. Tightening his grip on the handhold in the wall, he drew back his arm and threw.

He couldn't balance himself well enough to put a great deal of power behind the throw. He missed the snake and the rock dropped to the floor below.

"Kent, get it for me, will you?"

"Here." Kent picked up the rock and tossed it up to him. "But be careful, Bruce. You know how dangerous those snakes are!"

With all the strength Bruce could muster, he threw the rock again. This time it was accurate. It snapped the snake's head back against the rock. For an instant the ugly creature threshed wildly about before sliding off the ledge and dropping to the floor. Bruce saw it falling and shouted a warning.

"Look out, Kent!"

Kent sprang to one side as the snake thudded down almost at his feet. He started to climb the wall frantically, but the rattler slithered away in the darkness.

For a minute or so Bruce clung there breathing heavily.

"Wow, you took a chance," Kent exclaimed with admiration in his voice.

"The snake's gone now. That's the main thing."

"Let's hope there aren't any more of them up there," Kent said. There was a short pause before he spoke again. "I really wasn't afraid of that snake." His boasting had a hollow sound, but he continued – gaining strength and courage from his own words. "I didn't exactly come down because I was afraid of him. You see, I didn't have a knife to dig a rock out of the wall, so I dropped to get something I could use to throw. If you hadn't beaten me to it, I'd have been back up there in a couple of minutes and would've taken care of that old snake myself."

Bruce did not reply immediately but started to climb again. After a moment he looked down. "We'd better get a move on if we're going to get out of here."

"You can say that again." Kent started to climb too. He followed the handholds he and Bruce had made a few minutes before. Bruce was close to the opening that led out into the fresh, pure air.

"You'd better watch it, Bruce," Kent cautioned.

"There could be another snake around."

"There isn't," Bruce replied.

With that he hoisted himself out of the opening and up into the brilliant sunlight. A couple of minutes later Kent did the same. For a time, they crouched there numbly, blinking their eyes and breathing heavily.

"Thank You, Lord." There was respect and adoration in Bruce's voice. "Thank You for helping Kent and me to find the air shaft and to get past the rattlesnake without getting bitten and to get safely out of the mine."

Kent laughed carelessly.

"There's one thing you forgot," he said. A strange, mocking tone filled his voice.

"What's that?"

"You forgot to thank Him for the gold we've got in our pockets." He took a chunk of the ore out of his pocket and looked at it. It had a dull, bronze color. But when he turned it in the sunlight, there was a telltale glint to it. "You know, Bruce," he continued, "we'd better not say anything to anyone about this gold. We want to have the mine for ourselves."

Bruce did not answer him. He was looking down the mountain toward the entrance of the mine.

"Look at all those guys down there. They must've followed our tracks to the mine and are ready to go in and dig us out."

Kent laughed.

"I guess we weren't in as much danger as we thought." He paused momentarily. "Know what we should do, Bruce? We should hide up here and let 'em dig out all that rock in the cave-in. Then when they finally got over here to the air shaft, we'd really have the laugh on 'em! I can just hear old Bob Anders snort."

CHAPTER 13

FOOL'S GOLD

Bruce looked steadily into Kent's eyes.

"No sir," he said firmly. "We've already caused people enough trouble. We're not going to do anything like that."

"We wouldn't mean anything by it. It'd just be a joke."

"Some joke!" With that Bruce strode off down the mountain alone. For an instant Kent stared after him. When he saw that Bruce was not coming back, however, he ran after him. They were about a hundred yards from the mine entrance when one of the guys looked up and saw them.

"There they are!" he cried.

Bruce and Kent burst into a run. A few moments later they reached the searching party. The men and boys gathered around them talking and laughing excitedly.

For a time, Bob let it go on. When, at last, the talk began to lessen, he strode forward to stand before

Kent and Bruce. Cringing under his steady gaze, they looked up at him.

"I hope you're satisfied," he said coldly.

"Wh–wh–what do you mean?" Kent blustered. "We ain't done nothin'."

"You have completely disrupted the activities of the camp," Bob said. "You caused thirty-eight men to leave their work and come up here at considerable personal expense to look for you. We've all been without sleep or anything to eat. And some of the men have risked their lives in an effort to get the cave-in cleared out in a hurry."

Kent's lips quivered uncertainly.

"We–we're sorry about that," he said. "We didn't mean any harm."

The anger in Bob's eyes flashed. "No, Kent, you never mean any harm."

At that moment Bruce stepped up to Bob.

"Mr. Anders," he said, "I–I'd like to apologize to you and–and ask your forgiveness for causing all this trouble."

Bob surveyed him quizzically.

"That's a little late, isn't it, Bruce?" he demanded. "I told you the last time you broke the rules that you would be sent home on the next offense. Apparently, you thought I was fooling."

"We don't deserve anything else," Bruce continued. "We knew what we should do, but we broke the rules anyway. We should be sent home for what we've done."

Bob took a deep breath and shook off his weariness. "Bruce," he said, "I've never heard you talk quite this way before."

"Something happened to me down in the mine," Bruce announced. "I accepted Christ as my Savior."

Bob beamed.

* * *

The men who had assembled to search for the boys began to go back to their homes by ones and twos. Bob Anders had the rest of the boys break camp and head back down the mountain as soon as they could. Shortly after dark they rode into camp. Bob called Bruce and Kent aside.

"I have talked with Tom Channing," he said. "We're going to have to send you home."

"What about Walt and Lee?" Kent wanted to know.

"They'll be staying."

When he had finished and dismissed them, Kent laughed about it.

"He thinks he's hurting' us by sendin' us home," he said. "I'm tired of this stupid place anyway. The sooner we get out of here the better I'll like it."

Bruce did not feel that way and told Kent so.

"You can say all you want to, but I don't blame Bob for punishing us by sending us home. My dad'll skin me alive when I tell him what happened, but I guess I deserve whatever I get. We did break the rules even after we'd been punished once and warned of what would happen if we did it again."

Kent snorted.

"You're soundin' as bad as Lee and Walt and all the rest." He took a deep breath. "I can tell you one thing. They ain't goin' to get me back here next year." He grinned as he took a piece of ore from his pocket. "That is, unless I come back and buy the place. You ain't forgettin' we've found ourselves a gold mine, are you?"

"I don't even know what's right for us to do about that," Bruce said.

"Well, I'll tell you what's right," Kent flared. "You're goin' to keep your big mouth shut, and so'm I. That mine b'longs to the two of us – and nobody else."

* * *

That night old Doc Staughton came down to see the boys and tell them goodbye before they left. Everyone else was at the campfire service, but Bruce and Kent were in their cabin when Doc found them.

"I'm mighty glad you guys got out of that there mine OK," he said. "I don't mind tellin' you, I was gettin' a mite worried. Them old, abandoned mines just ain't safe."

Kent laughed nervously.

"It wasn't so bad."

Doc's expression grew even more serious.

"Well, I'm goin' to tell you both somethin'. Don't you *ever* do anything like that again. You coulda got yourselves trapped down there an' 'bout all we'd a-found in a couple of years woulda been a mess o' bones."

"But we didn't get trapped," Kent said arrogantly.

The old man's eyes narrowed, and for an instant or two they flashed heatedly.

"No, you didn't," he repeated. "I just reckon maybe the good Lord wanted to give you one more chance. Y'know, sonny, He does things like that sometimes b'cause He loves us so much He wants to give us every chance He can to go to heaven."

Kent squirmed uncomfortably but did not say anything.

Bruce was the one who spoke. "I'm a Christian now," he said simply.

"So I hear." A smile crossed the old prospector's grizzled face. "And the way I figgers, I reckon that makes this whole mess plumb worthwhile." He sat down on a chair across from them. For a minute or two nobody spoke. "There's one more thing I come over to talk to you about," he went on. "Thought maybe you'd like to know that I found my grandpappy's old mine and staked out my claim on it."

Kent's eyes widened, and anger flecked them.

"You can't do that! We found it first! It b'longs to Bruce and me!"

"You found it first?" Puzzlement clouded the wrinkled old face. "I never knowed you was in there. The way it looked to me, nobody'd ever been there since my grandpappy quit workin' it."

Kent bristled.

"Oh yes, you did. You were there when they were goin' to dig us out."

Briefly Doc stared at him. Then a smile cracked the seamed, weather-beaten face.

"You ain't talkin' 'bout the old Spangler mine, are you?" he asked. "You don't think my grandpappy's mine is the one you guys was trapped in?"

"What other mine would it be?" Kent snapped. "It's the only one close. And besides, we even found gold in it."

Doc laughed gently.

"You found gold in the Spangler mine? Now that would be somethin' for the book. There never was no gold down in the Spangler mine."

Kent's temper flared.

"Maybe you just *thought* there wasn't any gold down there. Did you ever happen to think we might've found it?"

"I s'pose I could be wrong about that old mine," Doc continued. "But iffen there's gold down there it'd sure s'prise me – an' anybody else who knew anything about that mine." He scratched his head thoughtfully. "You do sound mighty sure of yourself, sonny. You wouldn't by any chance have a sample of that there gold you found, would you?"

Kent eyed him suspiciously.

"I don't know whether we should show it to you or not. You just might try to steal it from us."

"I ain't never stole a claim in my life, sonny," Doc retorted, "and I don't aim to start now. I give you my word. If you found gold in that old shaft, I'll be right happy for you."

Kent hesitated, but Bruce fished a piece of the ore from his pocket and dropped it into the old man's hand. Doc eyed it gravely, a new light glinting in his faded blue eyes.

"Did you get this here out of the Spangler?" he asked quietly.

Kent broke in. "We sure did. Now do you think we're tellin' you somethin' that ain't true when we say there's gold in that mine?"

"You should've seen it shine when Kent accidentally turned the flashlight on it," Bruce said, laughing in his excitement. "It was really something!"

Doc chuckled.

"I'll bet you were excited at that. I've had my times that way too. See somethin' in the rocks and your old heart gets to hammerin' a mile a minute." The smile faded slowly. "But, boys, this here piece of ore is just like a lot of people you meet. It's phony clean through."

Slowly Kent and Bruce straightened.

"What do you mean?" Kent demanded harshly. "It's gold, ain't it?"

Doc shook his head.

"I wisht I could tell you that it's gold. B'lieve me, I do. It looks like gold. In fact, a lot of people mistake it for gold. But, to tell you the truth, it ain't nothin' more than iron pyrites."

"What's that?"

"Iron pyrites?" Doc repeated. "Fool's gold. It ain't worth nothin'. Nothin' at all."

Kent stared at Doc and then at Bruce. The lights died in his eyes.

"I–I thought–" he said weakly. "I thought sure it was–"

"You wouldn't find no gold in the old Spangler mine, sonny," Doc continued. "It's an old silver mine. 'Twas worked for almost forty years b'fore the ore petered out. They was plenty of silver in it, but there never was no gold down there."

Kent took the ore from his pockets and looked at it incredulously.

"You mean it ain't no good?" Kent repeated, as though he could scarcely believe it. "You mean it ain't worth nothin' at all?"

"Nope," Doc said. He started to chuckle again. "Iffen it was, you'd be lookin' at a billionaire. I've found myself a mountain of that stuff down through the years. It used to give me quite a thrill when I first seed it."

Bruce tossed his pieces of rock into a nearby ash can.

"I guess I never did really think we'd found anything that was goin' to make us rich."

"You guys don't know how bad I hated to tell you this," Doc said. "I've had 'nough disappointments in these here hills in my time, so I know how bad it makes you feel."

For a minute or two nobody spoke. Then Bruce turned to their guest.

"You said something about finding your grandfather's mine," he said. "Did you really find it, or were you just kiddin' us about that?"

"No sirree, I wasn't kiddin' nobody," Doc repeated. Once more he smiled faintly. "I finally found it."

"But where?" the boys wanted to know. Excitement gleamed once more in their eyes.

"I found grandpappy's old mine, all right," he said. "And wouldn't you know it? It wasn't more'n three or four hundred yards from the old Spangler mine."

"It was!" Kent cried. "We looked all around, and we didn't see nothin'."

"You ain't the only one. I'd been past there I don't know how many times. And I never seen it once 'til I was up there waitin' for Bob and the forest ranger to come and help dig you guys out."

He took a piece of ore from his pocket and handed it to them.

"Now, take a look at this, guys," he said. "This here's real gold ore."

Kent took the ore in his hand, noted the weight of it, and studied it carefully.

"Is this real gold?" he asked doubtfully.

"It sure 'nough is. High-grade stuff too. Ain't had time to have it assayed yet, but I know it's rich ore. The best I ever did see."

"But it just looks like an old piece of rock with some dark streaks in it."

"Them dark streaks is gold."

Kent stared at Doc with new appreciation.

"I'll bet you're excited findin' that old mine, ain't you?" he asked.

The light faded from the prospector's face.

"To tell you the truth," he said slowly, "I don't know whether I feel glad or sad 'bout findin' that mine."

"What do you mean?" Bruce put in quickly.

"I've been trampin' up an' down these here hills for fifty years lookin' for it," he said. "I jest don't hardly know what I'm goin' to do with my time now that I've found it!"

"Think of all the things you c'n do," Kent said. "Think of the things you c'n buy!"

There was a long silence.

"I don't reckon I know much of anything I need right now. I've got a good house to live in, plenty of grub, and warm clothes. There ain't much more a guy could want."

Kent stared at him.

"You must be kiddin'."

"I s'pose maybe they's a few things I'll get."

"Think of all the fun you c'n have with it," Kent went on.

"Yeh, I guess you're right." Doc chuckled again thoughtfully. "I guess a guy could have an awful lot of fun with a pile of money – just seein' the good he could do with it."

Kent shook his head as though Doc wasn't quite right mentally for some reason.

* * *

The following morning Bob took Tom and the boys to Colorado Springs. Bruce took the next bus out for Denver while Kent left for his home in Fairview.

Bob had called Danny, so he and Kay were down at the bus depot to meet Kent.

Kent got off brusquely and swaggered over to where Danny and Kay were standing.

"Hi, Kent," Danny said.

The boy only scowled at them.

"Hello," Kay said. But he ignored her greeting completely.

"You don't need to act so glad to see me," he said, sneering. "I know you ain't. I'll bet you wish I'd been lost down in that old mine."

Danny did not act surprised or disturbed.

"Kent, that isn't true," he said quietly. "We are glad to have you home, although I don't mind telling you that we're sorry that it had to be a couple of days early."

The boy's lips set into a sneer, but he did not reply.

"I tried to tell you before you left that Bob wouldn't stand for any breaking of the rules. And especially the rules about leaving the campgrounds."

"That's it! Preach to me! That's all I heard since we left here!"

They got his suitcase and the three of them went over to the Orlis car. Once they were on their way home Kay turned to him.

"Well," she said pleasantly, "how was camp?"

He glared at her.

"Just about as crummy as it could be!" he snarled. "Or did you want me to lie to you and tell you that it was just lovely and I'm dyin' to go back?"

"Now, Kent," Danny said, his voice growing stern. "That's no way for you to act. I don't want to have to start disciplining you as soon as you get home, but we can't have you acting so belligerent and disagreeable."

Kent directed his cold, impersonal stare at Danny.

"There you go! Yellin' at me again!"

* * *

That evening when Danny and Kay were alone, they discussed Kent and his attitude since he had returned from camp.

"I'm terribly disappointed," Kay said sorrowfully. "Kent isn't any better than he was when he left."

Danny nodded.

"I was so much in hopes that a summer at camp would change him," she went on.

"So was I. But we don't want to forget that Kent is just like every other person. He's a free moral agent. God will work in his life if he wants Him to. But if he's determined to hold onto his will and do exactly as he pleases, God will allow him to do so – even though it means Kent will likely *get* into a peck of trouble."

"I know that's right," Kay said. "And I suppose I

was looking for the easy way out. It would have been so much easier for us if he had come back a Christian."

"But we can't lose courage or faith just because things didn't work out that way. We'll just have to keep praying for him."

* * *

The next morning Kent got up at his usual time, did a few chores around the house, and went out to a nearby vacant lot where a group of guys his own age were playing ball.

"Hi," he said arrogantly.

They looked at him and spoke.

"When'd you get back?"

"You guys should've been with us," he bragged. "We went horseback ridin' every day and swimmin' and mountain climbin' and everything!" A superior grin twisted the corners of his mouth. "We even helped an old guy find the gold mine that had been his grandfather's. He's goin' to be a millionaire!"

The boys eyed him scornfully.

"If it hadn't been for us, he'd never have found it," he said. "He wanted to give us part of it. But we figgered he needed it worse'n we did, so we wouldn't let him."

"You don't expect us to b'lieve that, do you?" one of the boys asked.

"You don't have to b'lieve it if you don't want to. It doesn't make no difference to me!"

"I bet you never even got *near* a gold mine!"

"We did too! Just ask Tom Channing or Lee Nelson or Walt Thatcher when they get back. They'll tell you whether I'm givin' you the straight goods or not."

"I had a letter from Walt this morning," the boy went on. "He didn't say anything about it."

An odd, trapped look clouded Kent's eyes. For an instant or two he fumbled for an explanation.

"Walt prob'ly didn't say nothin' b'cause he was just jealous that he wasn't along. Bruce Mackay and me were the only ones who were in on it, so Walt and Lee were both awful jealous of us."

The other guy studied Kent.

"Are you tellin' the truth?" Admiration crept slowly into his voice.

Kent flushed.

"Sure, I'm tellin' the truth. If you guys want to hear all the things we did, I'll tell you sometime. We had ourselves a ball!"

The guys crowded closer about him.

"Give us the lowdown, will you?"

"I ain't got time right now." Turning, he swaggered away.

He'd show them! He'd show them all! At that moment Kent Gilbert felt as good as though all the things he had told the guys were actually true. They swallowed his story. That was enough for him. He crossed the street and turned the corner toward home.

THE *DANNY ORLIS* SERIES

The Danny Orlis series, by Bernard Palmer, delivers a blend of adventure, mystery, and suspense through various settings—from the Canadian wilderness to Guatemalan jungles. Danny Orlis, an adept outdoorsman, skilled athlete, and committed Christian, employs his quick thinking, calm bravery, and biblical solutions to confront everyday problems and hair-raising dangers. Early stories focus on Danny navigating school life, sports, and outdoor challenges, while in later books, Danny and his wife Kay provide wisdom and guidance to youngsters facing lifelike situations and challenges. Having sold over two million copies, this series has made Palmer a renowned author in Christian youth literature. Palmer is also the author of the Felicia Cartright series and various other series for Christian youth.

AVAILABLE FROM WWW.ANEKOPRESS.COM